The
Empty Mirror

The
Empty Mirror

James Lincoln Collier

BLOOMSBURY

BLOOMSBURY

Published by Bloomsbury, New York and London
Distributed to the trade by Holtzbrinck Publishers

Library of Congress Cataloging-in-Publication Data
Collier, James Lincoln.
The empty mirror / James Lincoln Collier.
p. cm.
Summary: Thirteen-year-old Nick, whose parents died in a 1918 flu epidemic,
must find out why his mirror-image is causing mischief around their
New England town and making sure Nick gets the blame.
ISBN 1-58234-949-5 (alk. paper)
[1. Ghosts--Fiction. 2. Influenza--History--Fiction. 3. Orphans--Fiction.
4. New England--History--20th century--Fiction.] I. Title.
PZ7.C678Em2004   [Fic]--dc22   2003065814

First U.S. Edition 2004
Printed in the U.S.A. by Quebecor World
1 3 5 7 9 10 8 6 4 2

Bloomsbury USA Children's Books
175 Fifth Avenue
New York, New York 10010

For Tim, Leo, and Kitty

Chapter One

Sometime just before daylight I had a real bad dream, and I woke up with my heart pounding. I lay there for a minute, trying to bring the dream back into my mind so I could understand it, but I couldn't. I went on lying there, filled with the feeling that I'd lost something very important, something I could never get back. The feeling was mighty strong. I kept trying to think what it might be, but I couldn't. Finally I couldn't stand feeling like that, and I got up.

I'd gotten feelings from dreams before. Usually they wore off pretty quick, and by the time I'd had breakfast the dream feeling was gone. But this time the dream feeling hung on. I couldn't shake it.

Being as it was Sunday, I didn't have to work at

our boatyard. Didn't have anything to do but my chores, go to church at eleven o'clock. Maybe get up a baseball game over at Briggs Pond with Tommy Barnes, Mike Santini, and some of the others.

Uncle Jack made codfish cakes for breakfast, the way he usually did on Sunday for a change from eggs or oatmeal. After breakfast he said he was going down to the boatyard for a while. Uncle Jack didn't like being idle, Sunday or no Sunday. It didn't sit comfortable with him. He said, "I want to straighten out a few things in the shop." Uncle Jack liked things tidy. We had everything you needed for boats in our shop except engines—marine paint, line, all kinds of hardware and fittings, caulking, whatever. I liked the tarry smell of it. You could always lay your hand on anything you needed. Uncle Jack believed in being tidy, all right. "I'll be back around ten-thirty," he said. "Clean yourself up before church. What're you going to do this morning, Nick?"

"Maybe I'll see if Barnes and Santini want to play baseball."

"Be ready for church," he said. Then he left.

But that dream was still on me, and I didn't feel much like playing baseball. I just wanted to get rid of that feeling, so I went out the kitchen door, crossed the backyard, and started off for the hills behind town. I did that sometimes when I wasn't feeling good. The hills were covered with pines, but there were places where a rock ledge broke out of the ground and opened up the pines. On a ledge you could see our little village down below, then the bay with the fishing boats leaving white stripes behind them. I liked being there and looking down on everything. It made me feel like a king on his throne.

I hiked up there, stood on a ledge, and looked down at the village and the bay. But that feeling was still on me. I didn't feel like a king, just a kid who had lost something important. I decided that if I had something to occupy my mind, I might feel better, so I walked down out of the hills, through the village to the boatyard. We had a little dock jutting fifty feet into the bay, the shop, and the yard where we worked on boats. Chain-link fence all around it. As I walked into the yard, Uncle Jack gave me a look. He was never mean to me, never shouted, even though I could be troublesome at times— cutting school, talking back. But I knew enough to watch out when he gave me that look.

"What?" I said.

"Where've you been, Nick?"

"Up in the hills. Up in the pines." I didn't mean to tell him about my feeling. "It was a nice day. I went for a walk."

Uncle Jack didn't say anything for a minute, but leaned on the big screwdriver he was using to pry the planks loose from the hull of a dory. He was thin, tall, wiry. His hair was gray, but neat. You never saw Uncle Jack with his shirttail out, no matter how hard he was working. Never wanted a shave—wouldn't even come to breakfast without shaving first. It came from being in the army during the war, I figured. He fought in France in 1918. He was in the Meuse-Argonne battle, they said. Did something brave and got a medal for it, but he wouldn't talk about it. A couple of times, I asked, but he always said, "Best to forget about those things, Nick." Uncle Jack came home from France in the winter of 1918 and found that my ma and pa had both died in the flu epidemic, two days apart, and that he had me on his hands. Twenty years old and he had a baby to raise.

"Miss Bell came by a little while ago. She said she saw you down by Briggs Pond a while ago. She said hello to you, and you looked right through her and walked on by without saying a word."

I stood there, still soaked with that funny feeling, and tried to remember when I'd been over to Briggs Pond. Not for a week, so far as I could remember—went over there with Gypsy last Sunday just for something to do. "When did Miss Bell see me?"

"A little while ago. Maybe an hour ago. She got to wondering if something was wrong with you, were you sick or something, and came by to ask."

Miss Bell would use any excuse to visit with Uncle Jack. Miss Bell wasn't my cup of tea. That was an expression I had. I liked having expressions for various things. They made me feel cheerful. Miss Bell ran the Ye Olde Pastry Shoppe, where you could get cake, tarts, and such. The fishermen hung out there sometimes when they were waiting out a storm. I have to say, Miss Bell made mighty good chocolate cake, even if she wasn't my cup of tea. She was always leaving a chunk of cake off for Uncle Jack. She was sort of pretty, although a little hefty, and sometimes acted in plays over at Millbury. She'd use any excuse to come by the house, and I figured this was another one. "Uncle Jack, I've been up in the pines. Nowhere near Briggs

Pond. She must have made a mistake."

"That isn't very likely, is it, Nick? She's known you since you were born."

I stood there looking at Uncle Jack, confused. It sounded like Miss Bell really did see me. She couldn't have made a mistake like that. Everybody in Stoneybeach knew everyone else. "Maybe she misremembered," I said. "Maybe it was last Sunday, when I was over there with Gypsy. Maybe Gypsy was talking and I didn't hear Miss Bell say hello."

"She said it was this morning. Hour or so ago. She couldn't have got that wrong, Nick."

Something was wrong somewhere. Miss Bell couldn't have made a mistake about who I was, not if I walked past her in broad daylight. But I wasn't there. "Uncle Jack, I wasn't there. I swear it. It had to be someone else."

He gave me a sideways look. For a minute he didn't say anything. Then he said, "Well, all right. I can understand if you had something on your mind and didn't hear her, but I don't like to see a thirteen-year-old boy disrespect a grown woman." He turned back to the dory. There was no point in arguing with him anymore, for he'd closed the subject.

It all bothered me a lot. First the feeling I'd lost something, and then Miss Bell seeing me when I wasn't there. I had to admit that Miss Bell knew me pretty well. I worked at her pastry shop sometimes, scrubbing floors and such. Had Miss Bell made the whole thing up for some reason? Was she trying to get me in trouble with Uncle Jack in case I tried to get between them? To tell the truth, I didn't think Uncle Jack was in any rush to marry anyone, especially Miss Bell. Maybe he was, but I didn't see any signs of it. Or did Miss Bell figure out she wasn't my cup of tea and wanted to get me for that?

It was bothersome, all right, and after church I decided to go see Gypsy Dauber. I could talk to Gypsy about anything. She liked to talk a whole lot, and it didn't much matter about what. The Daubers had a little farm back under the mountains. They were kind of mixed up. Gypsy said they were part Indian, which was probably true. Uncle Jack said from the name you'd take them for French-Canadian. Who knows what they were? It didn't matter to me. Gypsy and me didn't exactly fit in around Stoneybeach, she being mixed and me being an orphan. Oh, I had plenty of other friends—Mike Santini, Tommy Barnes, Joey Pileski, and such.

Their folks were always complaining that I was the one who got them in trouble—Mike and Tommy especially. Get them to cut school, borrow somebody's boat and go out to Goat Island to roast potatoes we'd swiped from Barnes's ma. Things like that. But when it came to being troublesome, Gypsy was always ahead of me. We got along real good.

I set off through the village and the dirt farm road that ran back toward the hills. The road wound through patches of oaks and maples. After that came the Daubers' farm—a scratchy little farm with a pig, a cow, a dozen chickens, and a truck garden with tomatoes, pole beans, melons, and such that they carted into Millbury in an old, broken-down Ford truck Mr. Dauber kept going with spit and haywire. I usually went out there to help them butcher the pig in the fall. It'd be a nice, sharp fall day with the leaves all red and yellow. Mr. Dauber would slice the pig's throat and let it run, the blood splashing out everywhere. It'd make maybe a hundred feet before it fell over on its nose. Mr. Dauber'd gut it out, and then we'd hoist it up with a pulley hanging from an arm that stuck out above their little barn door, dunk the carcass into an oil drum of hot water so as to soften the hairs, and then scrape it down with kitchen knives. I liked helping with the pig. Afterward Mrs. Dauber would give us apple pie and homemade cider that had turned a little and was fizzy. It was a mighty comfortable thing to do on a sharp fall Saturday morning.

Mrs. Dauber was sitting on the front porch out of the sun, stringing pole beans for supper. "Hello, Nick," she said. She was on the fat side, and lazy, always ready to take a glass of homemade cider and chat instead of getting on with her work.

"Mrs. Dauber, you know where Gypsy is?"

"She's in the barn shoveling out the cow stall if she knows what's good for her behind."

"I guess I'll have a look-see," I said. I went around the house, to the kitchen yard where the chickens were clucking around in the weeds and dust, looking for corn and seeds. "Shut up, you fools," I told them. "I'm king around here." Then I went on to the barn. The doors were slung wide open, which they usually were except in the worst weather, because the hinges were loose and the doors wouldn't close right. Gypsy came out of the barn carrying a loaded manure fork. She gave me a look, crossed the yard to the manure pile, heaved the forkload onto it, and crouched down, holding onto the manure fork to keep her balance. "How come I gotta work and you don't?" she said.

"It's Sunday. Uncle Jack doesn't make me work on Sundays."

I was trying to figure out how to bring up my bad feeling, and Miss Bell and all. Gypsy was likely to scorn you if you said something she thought was dumb. But I couldn't think of a safe way to bring it up, so I said, "I had a funny feeling all day. Then Miss Bell saw me when I wasn't there."

She stared at me, still crouching down, hanging on to the manure fork. "How could she see you if you wasn't there?"

"That's the whole point. She couldn't have, but she did."

Gypsy rose up. "I gotta finish the barn. You'll be able to tell me sooner if you help me."

"You haven't got but one manure fork," I said. "I know that for a fact." That was another of my expressions, knowing something for a fact. It had a heavy sound, like you were plunking a spike into a plank.

"You can use the coal shovel." So I did. We

finished manuring out the barn and then Gypsy snuck into the kitchen, filled a milk bottle with cider, and wrapped up a big chunk of blueberry pie in a piece of the *Millbury Gazette*. We went around front to where her ma was sitting with the colander of beans on her lap. "Me and Nick are going somewheres," she said.

"Did you finish the barn?" Mrs. Dauber said.

"Yeah."

"I hope so. Otherwise your pa'll give you what for."

I'd never heard that expression, giving somebody what for. I liked it. It had a ring to it, like smacking a fork on the edge of a table, and I resolved I'd learn it. "We finished up, Mrs. Dauber."

"Well, I trust you, Nick, more'n I trust whatshername. What've you got in that there newspaper, Gypsy?"

"Dead frog," Gypsy said. "Me and Nick are going to see if it comes alive again if we put it back into the water. Old Man Sneakers said it would."

Mrs. Dauber sniffed. "Old Man Sneakers wouldn't know a dead frog if it bit him on the nose. You be back in time for supper, Gypsy."

We walked along the dirt road toward the pine

hills, kicking at the dirt to see the dust puff up. After awhile we came to the edge of the pine forest, where the mountain began to slant up. Here there was a little path that went off into the woods. We went on in there until we came to our place—a little clearing where a big old tree had fallen. The sun came in and short, soft grass grew there. We sat on the trunk of the dead tree side by side so we could share the pie and cider. "So how come Miss Bell seen you when you wasn't there, Nick?"

"I don't know. She couldn't have, but she swears she did. Uncle Jack got on me about it. He said he didn't like to see a boy disrespect a grown woman."

Gypsy was staring at me with her eyes bright. She was getting interested. Gypsy liked things that were out of normal. "What about this feeling you had? Where'd that come from?"

"I don't know," I said. "It was there when I woke up this morning. Must have come on me in the night. I never had such a feeling before."

"What's it feel like, Nick?"

I thought about that, trying to come up with some way to describe it. "It's hard to say. I don't know if you can describe a feeling. It's—it's—like I lost something. Lost part of me and was going to get what for."

"I see you got a new expression," Gypsy said.

I blushed. She wasn't supposed to notice that. "You're not supposed to comment on people's speech."

"You're always telling me not to say *ain't*."

"Can't you ever not argue, Gypsy? This is serious. I won't tell you about it if you're going to argue."

"Okay, I won't argue. What else about it?"

"I went up into the hills to get rid of the feeling, but it didn't go away, so I came back down again. I went down to the boatyard. Uncle Jack said that Miss Bell saw me out by Briggs Pond awhile ago and that I walked on by her without saying hello or anything. Only I wasn't out by Briggs Pond—not since last week when we went out there."

Gypsy thought for a while, trying to think of some way I might have got it wrong. But she couldn't. "What else about it?"

"That feeling. It's got to come from someplace. I figure it comes from Miss Bell seeing me when I wasn't there."

"I don't know, Nick," Gypsy said. "I get feelings all the time that don't come from someplace."

"Probably they do come from someplace, only you don't know where."

"Why wouldn't I know where they come from? They're in me, aren't they?"

"You're arguing backwards against yourself, Gypsy."

"I don't care what you say, I get feelings I don't know where they come from lots of times."

I didn't want to fight about it. "It's a hard nut to crack, probably."

"Listen, Nick," she said. "Let's go out to the pond and see. Maybe we'll find some reason for it."

Suddenly I didn't want to go there. That was a strange thing, too. I'd been going out to Briggs Pond all my life. Swum in it in summer, skated on it in winter, played football and baseball in the fields around it hundreds of times. Briggs Pond was one of the main places in Stoneybeach for kids. Grown-ups were always saying some kid was going to drown in it someday, but so far nobody had.

Why was I scared to go out there? It didn't make any sense. But I was. "I don't know if we have time to get out there before supper."

"Sure we do, Nick. You ain't scared, are you?" Gypsy was always ready for anything that seemed like an adventure.

I couldn't stay away from Briggs Pond for the rest of my life. I stood up. "I'm not scared. Let's go."

We went along the path through the pines from our clearing to the farm road. The smell of pines in the hot sun was sweet and bright, but I was too nervous to enjoy it. Briggs Pond was about half a mile outside of Stoneybeach, a mile back from the beach. You could get to it either by the tar road that ran out of town toward Millbury, or by the path we were on, which ran through the farmland back of town. We walked on over. Gypsy did most of the talking. I let her; I was too nervous to want to talk.

Finally we came to Briggs Pond. It was about a hundred yards across, fed by a stream that ran down out of the mountain. There were fields all around it, except at the rear side, where it backed up against the piney hills. A hundred years ago somebody had dammed up the stream to make a millpond. The mill was long gone—burnt down a long time ago—but you could still see the remains of the foundation, where it had been.

There was nobody around. Might have been some kids there earlier in the day, but it was getting toward suppertime, and they'd gone home. There was still plenty of sun, though. We went across the field to the edge of the pond. My heart was beating thumpety-thump, and my legs felt shaky. I just couldn't figure out why I felt so scared.

Gypsy stood there looking around. "I don't see anything," she said.

"I told you so, Gypsy."

She looked at me as if she might see something interesting in my face. "You see anything special, Nick?"

"Nope," I said. Maybe the whole thing was nothing after all. Maybe my feeling was just a feeling. Maybe Miss Bell had been seeing things.

"Don't you remember anything, Nick?" She was getting disappointed. "Isn't something coming into your head?"

We wandered over to the edge of the pond and stood there looking around. Everything was normal—nothing different from the way it had always been. I looked down at the water. Because of the angle of the sun, it was hard to see through the water to the bottom. I lifted my eyes a little and looked toward the back of the pond. The wall of pine trees and the blue sky were reflected on the water there. I looked closely. There was more blue sky, and Gypsy's reflection.

Then my backbone went cold, and a chill rose up and shivered across my head. Gypsy's reflection was there, all right. But there was no reflection of me.

Chapter Two

For a moment I stood there, just staring. My mind was all woolly. I couldn't think; I could only stare down at the reflection of blue sky with a little white cloud in it, where I should have been. "Gypsy, I'm not there," I said in a whispery voice. "I'm not there."

"You ain't there, Nick." She turned her head to look at me, kind of awestruck, like I'd suddenly got famous. "Where'd you go to?"

I couldn't get hold of it. It was like I'd started melting or shrinking or something. I looked at her. "Gypsy, something's wrong. Something bad's happening to me."

She was staring at me. "Do you still have that bad feeling you woke up with this morning?"

I looked inside myself to see. "No. Well, yes, but it's different. Now I *know* there's something wrong with me."

"Do you feel like somebody else?"

"I'm still me, Gypsy. I'm not somebody else."

"That's good," she said. "I don't want you to be nobody else."

"I can't look anymore," I said. I stepped away from the edge of the pond.

"Me neither," she said. We didn't say anything for a minute. Then she said, "What're you going to do, Nick?" She wasn't looking so awestruck now—more worried that I might become dangerous to her. "You gotta do something."

I looked up at the sky, kind of hoping to see an answer up there. There was nothing but blue sky and a couple of small clouds. "I don't know what to do. I don't know if there's anything I can do. Something's happening to me that I haven't got any say over."

"Maybe it'll go away," she said. "Maybe when you wake up in the morning, it'll be gone. It came in the night, maybe it'll go in the night."

"I don't know," I said. "I got my doubts." Using an expression didn't cheer me up. I thought for a minute. "Maybe I better go talk to Miss Bell. Maybe she could tell me something. Maybe it was my reflection she saw here this morning."

"You think it was your reflection that walked by her without saying hello?"

"Gypsy, don't be crazy."

"Then you explain it. Miss Bell's probably lying anyway."

I looked at the sun dropping down toward the hills. Most times looking at the sun shining on the pines gave me a real nice feeling, but not now. "We better get home, Gypsy. We're going to be late for supper." We walked away from the pond across the field, not saying anything until we got to where the tar road into town branched off from her path. Here we stopped. "Nick, soon as something happens, tell me. If your reflection comes back in the morning, tell me."

"Uncle Jack won't let me get away from the boatyard. We've got a lot of work coming in."

"Say you're sick."

"I don't think it'll come back that easy."

She grabbed my hand. "Yes it will, Nick. I promise. It'll be back. It'll be back in the morning." Then we headed for home.

I would be late for supper and wouldn't have any good excuse. Uncle Jack was already down on me for disrespecting Miss Bell. But he wouldn't be too hard on me. He never was. I guess he figured it wasn't right to be too hard on an orphan.

Uncle Jack had gotten his own share of hard luck out of it, for he'd had to take me in before he was hardly grown up himself. He wouldn't ever complain about it—never. That wasn't Uncle Jack's way. He always took what came and never complained. But other people in Stoncybeach let me know. If I ever complained about Uncle Jack—said he was too tidy or worked me too hard—they'd tell me I had no business complaining: Uncle Jack took me in when a lot of other young fellows wouldn't have.

The war changed Uncle Jack, they said. He'd gone off in 1917 full of patriotism. He'd been hit by hand-grenade shrapnel in the Battle of Meuse-Argonne. He'd crawled halfway across no-man's-land, dragging his buddy out who'd gotten hit bad, the machine guns slashing at him, and him bleeding from his arm. It wasn't until he got back into his own trenches that he realized he'd been dragging a corpse. He passed out there. He was lucky he lived. They sent him back to England to a hospital. Uncle Jack never told me any of this, but a man from Millbury was in his outfit and saw it. Uncle Jack had a medal for it, the man said, but I'd never seen it.

When he came back from the war, he was changed, they said. Before, he'd been the jolly type, chasing after the girls and always ready for a laugh. So they said, anyway. He got serious from the war and my pa and ma dying in the flu epidemic. Miss Bell was always telling him he lived inside himself too much. I guess anybody who'd dragged the corpse of his buddy across no-man's-land was likely to live inside himself. You didn't have to worry about Miss Bell living inside herself, that was for certain.

When I came in from Briggs Pond, Uncle Jack was already at the old wooden table eating his supper. He looked at the big old wall clock that made a tick-tock like a tongue clicking. "Six o'clock," he said.

"It wasn't my fault," I said. "I went over to Briggs Pond with Gypsy to figure out how Miss Bell could have seen me there."

"Don't see what there was to figure out," he said.

"You must have been woolgathering. It's not like you were never known to woolgather before. Help yourself to supper. There's stew on the stove and some oatmeal bread in the oven." Uncle Jack wasn't any fancy cook, but he did good enough.

I liked being in our kitchen. The house was pretty much like most of the houses in Stoneybeach: two bedrooms upstairs; parlor, kitchen, bathroom downstairs. Nothing fancy: iron stove in the kitchen, some painted cupboards, old wooden table. In the parlor an old leather horsehair sofa that had come from my grandpa's house, couple of chairs, photos of Grandpa and Grandma, photo of Ma and Pa dressed up for their wedding, table with a lamp on it so you could read on the horsehair sofa if you could figure out a way to keep from sliding off.

The parlor was too gloomy. The kitchen was more cheerful, especially in the winter when the stove was hot and the sun streamed in. I did my homework in the kitchen during the winter because the heat took its time getting upstairs to my room, and when it did get there, it wasn't what you'd call heat anymore.

I got a dish of stew and a couple of slices of bread and sat down at the table. "I reckoned I'd go see

Miss Bell and talk to her about what happened." I wanted to see what I could find out.

"It wouldn't go amiss to apologize," Uncle Jack said.

I sure wasn't going to apologize for something I hadn't done. "I'll talk to her about it."

Uncle Jack gave me a look, but he didn't say anything. Instead, he got up, put his dishes in the sink for me to wash later, and went out into the parlor to read the *Millbury Gazette*.

He didn't believe me. I sat there eating my stew and thinking. What if I took him into the bathroom and showed him in the mirror that my reflection was gone? He'd have to believe me then. But I didn't want to do it. I didn't want anyone to know about it. Everything about it was strange, and I didn't want people to think I was strange. Being an orphan was bad enough. I knew it wasn't my fault that my ma and pa had died in the flu epidemic, but somehow I kept feeling that it was. Same with the reflection: I couldn't see where it was my fault that I had lost mine, but I still didn't want people to know about it. I could only hope that I'd wake up in a couple of days and be back to normal.

I guess I wouldn't have felt bad about being an

orphan but for the way people acted about the influenza epidemic. Nobody ever talked about it—they acted like it had never happened. There was some kind of dirtiness to it. But I was curious, and when I was around ten I told our teacher, Miss Quince, that I wanted to do a report on it. She said it was better to leave things like that alone, but I wouldn't give up, and finally she said she would drive me over to Millbury, where they had a library. I spent an afternoon looking it up in a book the librarian found for me.

It started in August 1918. It was terrible. Forty million people died from the flu worldwide, the book said, and maybe a whole lot more—they were dying so fast nobody could keep count of them. Some places the undertakers wouldn't go near the dead, and made parents bury their children and husbands bury their wives. Other places the coffins were stacked up along the roads leading to the cemeteries because there were too many to bury. They died by the ton. A couple of times, over in France, battles were called off because the soldiers were too sick to fight. That seems hard to believe, but it was so.

It finally crept up to Millbury and then to

Stoneybeach that October. It hit all at once like a tornado. One day everybody was fine; four days later they started to die. It seemed for a while like half the town was sick. They died and died and died. The school closed, then the churches, and then the stores, because nobody wanted to go out on the streets. Those who had to go out covered their faces with gauze so they wouldn't breathe in germs.

Six weeks later it was over. Gone, like it had never been there. But 106 out of 600 and something in Stoneybeach were dead. Two of them were my ma and pa. Uncle Jack got home a week after they were buried. I wasn't but eleven months old. The minister was keeping me in the basement of the church, along with four other little kids who had been left orphans. Uncle Jack, he was only twenty and still had his arm in a sling, but he said he would take me, it was his duty. And so he did. Never told me it was his duty, always said he was glad to have me, but other people told me I should be grateful. There's always somebody around who knows what you should be grateful for. They said if Uncle Jack hadn't taken me in, I'd have been shipped off to an orphanage, fed on cornmeal mush, and whipped regular. It didn't occur to them that I might have gotten adopted by a rich millionaire, lived in a mansion, had my own pony, and eaten pie and ice cream for breakfast. People who know what you should be grateful for never think of such things. I knew they were right, I should be grateful, and I tried. Being grateful didn't come easy to me, but I did my best.

It could have been a whole lot worse. I could have had somebody like Gypsy Dauber's pa, who was always coming home drunk, shouting and cursing, and taking a whack at Gypsy if she didn't get out of the way fast enough. Uncle Jack was honest and fair. And every once in awhile he'd look at me like he'd just realized I was there and say, "Nick, we've been working too hard the last little while. I reckon we might take a day off and go fishing." We'd get out our dory with its leg-o'-mutton sail, go out onto the bay and loll around in the sun. Or we'd drive the truck over to Millbury, take in a movie, and have an ice cream soda afterward. Times like that it wasn't so hard to be grateful.

I finished off my supper. Being scared so much made me hungry, but at the same time it made me feel full. I got up, washed the dishes, dried them, and put them away. Then I went out into the parlor. "I'm going over to Miss Bell's," I said.

Uncle Jack pulled out his pocket watch. "Six-thirty. She'll be closing the shop by now, I reckon."

"She'll be out back cleaning up, most likely." I left the house and started over. The sun was dropping behind the hills, and red rays slanted through the narrow streets. I was sick of having that bad feeling, and as I went along I tried to convince myself that there wasn't anything wrong with having no reflection. So what if I didn't have any? Nobody has reflections most of the time— not unless they're standing in front of a mirror, a shop window, a pond. What difference did it make? But I couldn't convince myself: there was something wrong with you if you didn't have a reflection.

It was only ten minutes over to Miss Bell's. The shop was locked and the lights were out, but a light was coming from the back room where the bakery oven, pastry table, and such were. I rapped on the glass of the door. "Miss Bell, it's Nick Hodges." I figured that'd fetch her, for she'd hope Uncle Jack had sent me over with an invitation for her to come up and play cribbage with him like she did sometimes. I was right; in a minute she came out of the back room, wiping her hands on her apron. She was a blondish woman around Uncle Jack's age, pretty enough if you didn't mind a little pudginess here and there. She unlocked the door and swung it open.

"Hello, Nick. Nothing wrong with Jack, is there?"

"No, he's fine." I stepped in and closed the door behind me, feeling nervous. "I wanted to find out—I mean, what happened at Briggs Pond this afternoon?"

"Well, I must say, it did surprise me that you would walk by without speaking."

I was sure now that she was worried I was trying to get in the way of her marrying Uncle Jack. "See, the thing is, Miss Bell, I would have said hello, only I wasn't there. I was up in the pine forest right then."

She frowned down at me. "I must say I'm surprised, Nick. I know you have a reputation for being troublesome. A lot of folks around here blame you for leading their kids into trouble. Cutting school. Taking boats that don't belong to you."

"We did that only twice. We brought the boats right back."

"Still, it wasn't right. People generally forgive you, for they believe you've got a good heart and only need the firm but loving hand of a woman to steady you. I don't know how often I've told Jack you need a woman's touch to steady you, but you know Jack, he's stubborn as a mule. Troublesome, Nick, but I never knew you for a liar."

"I'm not a liar, Miss Bell. I wasn't there. Maybe you misremembered. Maybe you didn't have your glasses on and it was some other kid."

Her frown was pouring down all over me. "I know I wear glasses, but that's only for close work. You weren't but five feet from me, Nick. I could have reached out and touched you." She went on pouring her frown on me. "You're up to something, aren't you, Nick? You and Gypsy Dauber, no doubt."

She bent down so her face was level with mine and close, and stared into my eyes, the way grown-ups do when they're going to lie to you. She put her hands on my shoulders. "Nick, I wish you'd tell me what it is. I'm sure it's not nearly so bad as you think. I won't say anything to Jack. We'll work it out together."

The easiest thing would have been to tell her I was at Briggs Pond, say I was thinking about my ma and pa being dead or something and didn't want to speak to anybody. Tell her I was sorry and wouldn't do it again. But I wasn't going to. I wasn't going to take the blame for something I hadn't done. Besides, working it out together was a big lie. She'd shoot over to our house like a bullet the first minute she could to spill it to Uncle Jack as a good example of what a woman's firm but loving hand could do. "Miss Bell, I don't care what you think. I wasn't at Briggs Pond this morning."

She turned beet red. "I hope you aren't calling me a liar, Nicholas Hodges. You better think things over a little. People around here have been patient with you, but their patience is wearing thin. You go on home now and have a little chat with your-self." She swung the door open, and the next minute I was outside in the slanting orange rays of the sun, which came like arrows down the little streets of the town.

I walked on home, wishing I hadn't been so troublesome. I'd always liked being troublesome—wouldn't have done it if I hadn't liked it. But now I could see it wasn't going to be helpful. Besides, it wasn't always me who started the trouble. It was Tommy Barnes's idea to take Widow Wadman's goat over to the dump to see if it'd eat tin cans the way they said goats did. Cutting school was usually Gypsy's idea. She didn't have any use for school at all. "What's the point of it?" she said. "Who cares where Bermin is?"

"Berlin," I told her. "Maybe you'll want to go there someday."

"Naw, I wouldn't never want to go to no Bermin. Nothing but Irishers there."

"Germans," I said.

"Irishers, Germans, who cares? Who cares what half of a quarter is? I don't believe there is any such thing, anyway. How could you make a quarter into a half? A half is bigger than a quarter, ain't it?"

"Don't be so dumb, Gypsy," I said. "That isn't the idea of it at all. Suppose four of us got hold of one of your ma's blueberry pies and took it out into the woods. Naturally, we'd cut it into equal pieces, and—"

"Not if Mike Santini was cutting. He'd take half for hisself."

"Never mind Santini. We didn't bring him along."

"If he heard there was blueberry pie in it, he'd of

come along of his own accord."

"Why do you always argue about everything? I'm trying to explain something. Santini didn't find out. Now—"

"He would of found out. He can smell blueberry pie a mile away."

"How can I explain it if you keep bringing up Santini?"

"I don't want it explained at me, anyway."

I gave up. Anyway, you can see that Gypsy wasn't much of a one for school. I wasn't so sure, myself. Uncle Jack said you needed to do good at school if you were to get anywhere in life. He said he couldn't run the boatyard if he didn't know how to figure what such and such a job would cost, so he would know how much to charge. Couldn't shape a hull if he didn't know something about geometry. Or take the fishermen. Maybe they didn't have to know algebra, but they sure had to know how to read a map, calculate weights and measures, all about the stars. So I reckoned there might be something to school. Still, when Gypsy got it into her head to cut, I usually went along, which was stupid, for the minute Miss Quince saw we were both missing, she knew what was up.

Not that we cut every day. Or even every week. Every couple of weeks was more like it. But we did it more than most kids. And speaking up. Gypsy was a great one for speaking up. I liked to do it, too. I didn't get nasty about it and curse, nothing like that. But I liked speaking up now and again. If you decide to speak up, you can always find something to speak up about. You know, if somebody says, "A stitch in time saves nine," you can always get a good argument about that. How come it saves nine? Why not three or sixteen? And such. Or if they say, "It's an ill wind that blows nobody good," you can ask how the wind got ill, or bring up hurricanes. There's always an excuse to speak up, and I liked doing it.

Now I could see that I oughtn't have spoken up, or cut school so much, for once you got a reputation for being troublesome, people would believe anything bad about you, even if it wasn't really believable.

And now, on top of being troublesome, I had this strange thing happening to me. I couldn't get away from it. When I brushed my teeth that night in our little bathroom off the kitchen, all I saw in the mirror was the bathroom door with its towel racks behind me. I couldn't stand it, and I closed my eyes until I finished brushing. What would people say if I happened to get near a mirror and they saw I wasn't making a reflection?

I hated the idea of anyone knowing I was strange. I tried to remember where there were mirrors I might bump into. Big one in Ted's Barbershop. What was I going to do if Uncle Jack decided I needed a haircut, which he did pretty frequent to keep me tidy? There were mirrors in bathrooms at school, church, the village hall. I could probably manage to stay away from those. What else? Shop windows. You didn't always make a reflection in shop windows, but sometimes you did. Probably if I walked past windows quickly, nobody would notice. So I had some hope that I could keep people from finding out I didn't have a reflection. But *I* knew. Who wants to go around knowing there's something strange about themselves?

For the next two or three days I stayed pretty quiet—kept away from shop windows, turned my head down when I went into the bathroom. In my spare time away from the boatyard I spent a lot of time in my room reading Oz books Uncle Jack had got me for birthdays and Christmas. There wasn't much of interest to my room—painted chest of drawers, chair with a rush seat, little bed with a quilt that my ma had made before she married Pa. I liked having Ma's quilt. Sometimes when I wasn't feeling too good I'd hold the quilt close to my face so I could smell it, hoping some of her smell was still on it. Wasn't ever sure that there was, but I thought so.

To add some interest to the room I'd put up a couple of pictures from calendars. Calendars weren't any use once the year was over, and Uncle Jack didn't mind if I cut them up. I had a picture of a fat lady from a circus, dressed up in white boots, pantaloons, spangles, so fat she took up a whole sofa. Also a comical picture of a goat on a garbage heap eating a big beef stew can. Uncle Jack didn't mind about the goat, he said there wasn't anything wrong with goats, but the first time he saw the fat lady, he gave me a look. "Why on earth would a boy your age want a picture of a fat lady like that?"

"I don't know," I said. "I like to look at her." It was interesting to think what it felt like to be so fat you filled up a whole sofa.

The only person I could talk to about being

strange was Gypsy. I sure wasn't going to tell Santini or Pileski or Barnes. I was desperate to talk, so after supper one evening I walked out to her farm to see her. She was in the kitchen with her ma, playing hearts. Mrs. Dauber was a great one for hearts. She looked at me when I came in. "You want to play hearts, Nick?" she said.

I wanted to talk to Gypsy. "I'm not any good at hearts, Mrs. Dauber."

She sighed. "I never can get a good game around here. Gypsy gets restless with it."

"Hearts is boring," Gypsy said.

Mrs. Dauber threw down her cards. "Then you and Nick can darn well do the chickens."

We got a bag of chicken feed out of the barn. The chickens came clucking around. Instead of scattering the feed, Gypsy flung it at the chickens. They didn't seem to care.

"You fools," I said. "Don't you have any brains at all?" They didn't mind how I talked to them, either.

Then we looked around for their eggs, which they were just as likely to lay in the grass as in their nests in the chicken house. After we finished with that, we went behind the barn and sat there with our backs against the wall, chewing on long grass.

"What're you going to do, Nick?"

I thought about it. "That's what I can't figure out. For a while there I thought maybe Miss Bell was trying to get me in trouble with Uncle Jack so I wouldn't tell him not to marry her. But I don't think that anymore. She believes she saw me."

"Is your uncle Jack really going to marry Miss Bell?"

"I don't think so. I hope not. He doesn't seem to be of a mind to marry anybody. If he'd wanted a firm but loving hand over me, he'd have found someone to marry a long time ago. Too late for that now." I pushed my hair back. "I wouldn't mind if he did, so long as it wasn't Miss Bell. Maybe it'd be okay to have some wife around there. But I don't think getting married is Uncle Jack's cup of tea. He likes to be alone by himself a lot. That isn't what worries me. What worries me is being strange. No reflection. Being seen places where I wasn't. Something's wrong, Gypsy."

"Maybe it's the wood spirits, Nick. They do stuff like that."

I gave her a look. "There isn't any such thing as wood spirits."

"Oh yes there is, Nick. I seen 'em. Plenty of times. They come out just when it's getting dark. About a foot high and move so fast you can hardly get a look at 'em. One came into my room through the window one night. I seen it in the moonlight. Raced across my bed and out the door before I could catch ahold of it. Scared the pants off me."

"You sure you weren't dreaming?"

"Naw, I wasn't dreaming. Was wide awake. Saw it plain as day. Could be wood spirits, Nick."

I didn't feel like arguing about it. "I got to do something. I don't know what. Was Miss Bell seeing things? What could she have seen?"

"Well, that's clear enough, Nick. She seen your reflection. It was still there on the water. She thought it was you."

In the back of my mind I had known all along I'd have to think about that. I just hadn't been ready to. Didn't want to admit that such a thing could be. "I thought about that, Gypsy. It couldn't happen. I've never, ever heard of a single example where it happened before." I turned to look at her. "Did you ever hear of it?"

"That doesn't mean it couldn't happen. Maybe we just never heard of it."

"No, when you walk away from a mirror or something, your reflection disappears. Vanishes. Gone with the wind."

"Maybe this time it got stuck on Briggs Pond and Miss Bell come along and seen it."

"Don't be crazy, Gypsy. And don't give me anything about wood spirits." I looked at the sky. "It's getting dark. Uncle Jack'll start wondering. I better go."

So I walked on home through the growing darkness, watching the lights come on in the village, until I got to our house. I went in. Rev. Clampett was sitting at the kitchen table with Uncle Jack. That was kind of surprising: Uncle Jack went to church fairly frequently, but that was mostly because he figured I ought to go. He wasn't a particular friend of Rev. Clampett. I stopped dead in the kitchen doorway, knowing for a fact that a new bad thing had happened. They both stared at me. "What?" I said.

"Where've you been, Nick?" Uncle Jack said.

"Why? I was at Gypsy's."

There was a little silence. Then Rev. Clampett said in a high voice, "Nick, I saw you not a half hour ago. You were throwing stones at the church.

You broke six windows before I heard it in the parish house and came out. I know it was growing dark, but you ran through the light from the kitchen window, hardly an arm's length from where Mrs. Clampett was sitting. It was you, all right, Nick."

Chapter Three

I stared at them, first one, then the other. The world seemed to be spinning around me, and I put my hand on the doorjamb. Maybe I was going crazy. Was I dreaming when I believed I'd just come from Gypsy's? "I didn't, Uncle Jack. I was at Gypsy's. You can ask her." I realized I was shouting and trembling. I tried to calm myself down. "Ask Mrs. Dauber. She saw me. I was at the Daubers', I swear it."

There was silence, and then Rev. Clampett said in his high voice, "Sit down, Nick." He was a scraggly man with a long head and thin hair combed over his bald spot. He always wore a black suit like he'd just come from a funeral.

I knew what was coming, a whole lot of grown-up baloney. I wasn't going to sit down, though, so I went on standing in the doorway. Uncle Jack got himself a cup of coffee from the pot on the stove and stood back against the wall, half in the shadows.

"Nick," Rev. Clampett said, "something's bothering you, isn't it? Something's troubling you that you don't want to tell anyone about. Something you did, or thought, or that happened to you." He smiled a friendly smile. "I'm right, aren't I?" He went on smiling.

It was the kind of smile grown-ups put on when they figure they've got you dead to rights. "No. Nothing's bothering me." I was bound and determined they wouldn't talk me into admitting something that wasn't true.

Rev. Clampett went on smiling. "Nick, we *know* something's bothering you," he said in his high voice. "Yes, I'm aware that you can be mischievous. I've blamed that on your circumstances, which are hard for a boy. I don't think your friendship with Gypsy Dauber has helped, either. But this is more than mischief. We don't want to punish you. We think you'd feel a lot better if you'd tell us about it."

"I swear, Reverend Clampett, I didn't throw

stones at the church. I was out at Gypsy's the whole time." But who had done it?

Uncle Jack was holding his coffee mug in both hands. He didn't move out of the shadows but said, "Nick, people have overlooked a lot of things, but they can't overlook this. You've got to tell Reverend Clampett why you did it."

"I *am* telling you the truth," I shouted. "I *am* telling you. I didn't do it. That's the truth."

Rev. Clampett looked at Uncle Jack. Uncle Jack shrugged. "He'll have to work it off," he said. "He'll come up Sunday afternoons until it's worked off."

Rev. Clampett nodded. "I'm sorry, Nick. It would be a lot better for everybody if you told us what this was all about."

They weren't going to believe me. Nothing I said would matter. I folded my arms across my chest and stared at the wall, saying nothing.

"I think it would be a good idea if he stayed away from the Dauber child," Rev. Clampett said.

I unfolded my arms and balled up my fists. "That isn't fair," I shouted. "Gypsy didn't have anything to do with it."

"I'm sorry, Nick," Uncle Jack said.

That was the worst part. Gypsy was the only one I could talk to. People in Stoneybeach were beginning to give me funny looks when they saw me on the street or came into the boatyard. I figured they were talking—people always do. Saying I'd gotten worse, was going to the bad, even that I was going crazy. I didn't know they were saying such stuff for a known fact, but I reckoned they must be—it was what I would have done in such a case. So there wasn't anybody I could talk to about it except Gypsy. And now I wasn't supposed to visit her any more.

There was more to it than that. The truth of it was, maybe I was going crazy. First Miss Bell had seen me where I wasn't, and now Rev. Clampett and Mrs. Clampett both. They couldn't all be wrong, could they? Had I busted those windows after all and plain wiped it out of my mind?

It gave me a terrible feeling, like I wasn't myself anymore, like weeds and little bushes were growing inside me. I had to find the truth of it; I just had to. And that meant going out to the Daubers' and asking Gypsy and her ma if I really had been at their house at the time Rev. Clampett saw me throwing stones at the church. I just had to go there.

But I wasn't supposed to visit Gypsy. A couple of days went by and it came to Sunday. I went up to the church after our noon dinner. Rev. Clampett set me to cleaning out the graveyard behind the church. "It hasn't been cared for properly, Nick," he said. "I've been meaning to have something done about it for a long time." The graveyard was surrounded by rough stone walls. Behind the back wall was a stand of hardwoods, mostly oaks and maples. Farther back was the pine forest rising into the hills. I used to go up to the graveyard sometimes to look at the graves of my ma and pa, especially when I was feeling kind of down. I tried to pretend I knew them—knew how they talked, what kind of people they were. Was Ma jolly, or more the quiet type? Was Pa tidy like Uncle Jack? Ma was probably jolly, I'd decided, and Pa not so quiet and tidy as Uncle Jack. They were always laughing with each other. Looking at their graves made me sad, for I missed them a lot; but it comforted me when I was feeling down.

But I had work to do and couldn't get into a mood over it. It was a nice day—sun glinting on the oak leaves, little breeze blowing. I could have thought of worse places to be.

The graves needed a good deal of work. Some of them had been tended pretty well by the relatives—grass trimmed around the gravestone and flowers laid out—but a lot of them hadn't been touched. Relatives all dead, or moved away, or didn't care. I didn't mind helping those dead people out—kind of liked it. They'd have been pleased if they'd known about it. So I sickled the grass, trimmed, pulled up dandelions, weeded the paths, the sun on my back. It took my mind off my troubles.

But I had to know the truth of where I was when they saw me stoning the church, so one evening after supper I told Uncle Jack that Rev. Clampett wanted me to polish some church candlesticks, and I went on out to Gypsy's.

It was coming up to seven, and growing dark. I went around to the back of the house and in the kitchen door. Mrs. Dauber was sitting at the kitchen table, eating a slice of pie. "Gypsy's out back doing the chickens," she said with her mouth full.

"Okay," I said. "Mrs. Dauber, do you remember me coming up to visit Gypsy last week? Wednesday, I think it was."

She frowned. "I can't recollect exactly, Nick. You come up often enough. Usually half a pie missing when you go."

I let the pie rest. "You were playing hearts with Gypsy."

"We was having a nice game of it, too, until you showed up looking for pie. First time I got Gypsy to play with me for a month of Sundays."

I could have jumped and sung, but all I did was smile. "You can vouch for that? It wasn't some other time?"

"First time I got Gypsy to play with me for a coon's age, and you spoiled it, looking for pie."

So I wasn't crazy after all. "I wasn't looking for pie, Mrs. Dauber. I don't mind a piece of pie, but I wasn't looking for it."

"Well, you ain't getting any pie, Nick. I'm tired of feeding the whole neighborhood pie."

It wasn't the whole neighborhood, just me and Gypsy, but that was probably enough. "Where's Gypsy?"

"Doing the chickens, if she knows what's good for her behind."

"I'll go help her," I said.

Gypsy was out in the kitchen yard, flapping her skirt at the chickens to shoo them into the henhouse for the night. Foxes were bound to get them if you left them out at night. "I seen you in the kitchen. What were you talking to Ma about?"

"You heard what happened?"

"I heard you was caught breaking windows in the church. I knew it wasn't you. You was here. I told Ma so, I said, Nick didn't do it, but she said Reverend Clampett seen it plain as day."

That clinched it. "That's what I was talking to your Ma about. She said she was having a good game of hearts with you and I interrupted it."

"I'm bored with hearts. How come you didn't come up before?"

"Reverend Clampett said I wasn't to see you. He said it wasn't any help for me to be friends with you."

She frowned. "Them people. They don't like us anyway. Bunch of stuck-up snobs."

That was partly true, but partly it was the Daubers' own fault. If they'd cleaned up their yard a little and Mr. Dauber hadn't been drunk half the time, people wouldn't have been such snobs about them. Uncle Jack always said that people around Stoneybeach liked to live tidy. I couldn't say any of that to Gypsy, for she'd start throwing things at me. "I can't talk when you're flapping your skirt like

55

that." I gave one of the hens a little push with my foot. "Get in there, you fools. I'm king and you have to do what I say." Finally we got them locked in for the night, and then we went around behind the barn, a good distance from the manure pile, and sat there with our backs against the boards, watching the pines grow dark on the hills.

"The thing is, Gypsy, that time when Miss Bell said I walked past her without saying hello, you could figure she made a mistake. Saw somebody else or something. But this time it's too much of a coincidence. There's something—somebody—out there imitating me."

"Did you get your reflection back?"

"No."

"That's it, then. It's your reflection that done it. It escaped from you and is causing trouble."

"How could a reflection escape? That doesn't make any sense, Gypsy. Reflections can't climb out of a mirror and start walking around. Anyway, a reflection's flat. Turn it sideways and you can't see it."

"Maybe if a reflection escapes, it can become a whole person."

"Gypsy, be sensible."

She looked at me. "Well, then, who was it?"

I didn't say anything for a moment. Then, "That's the big question, isn't it? That's what we don't know."

"How're you gonna find out, Nick?"

I shrugged. "At least now I know I'm not crazy. Your ma saw me up here that time—she said so. And you know I was here."

"I know, Nick. I never believed you threw stones at no church."

She was on my side. She was the only one. "I got to go. Otherwise Uncle Jack'll get suspicious."

"Cheer up, Nick. At least you ain't dead."

"Not yet, anyway," I said. Then I started for home.

Talking with Gypsy had cheered me up a good deal. She was on my side, but more than that, I was sure now that I wasn't crazy. Sure that I'd been out there at the Daubers' when whoever it was—whatever it was—had busted the church windows. They were wrong, all of them: Rev. Clampett, Uncle Jack, Miss Bell, all the people around town who were talking about me. I was right, and I was determined to stand up to them. I didn't know where that would get me, but it would make me feel better.

Uncle Jack was sitting on the sofa in the parlor in a little circle of light from the lamp, reading the

Millbury Gazette when I came in. He put the paper down. "Where've you been, Nick? I saw it was getting late, so I went over to the church looking for you."

I stood by the door, wondering what I was in for. "I went over to see Gypsy Dauber."

"I figured that. At least you didn't lie about it." He folded up the paper.

"She's the only one I've got to talk to. I have to have somebody to talk to."

In the circle of light from the lamp he frowned, looking sort of puzzled, first down at the ground and then back at me. "I figured you could have talked to me about it."

I stood there looking at him. "You never talk about anything unless it's the weather or the price of cleats and shackles." I'd never spoken to him like that before.

He sat still, frowning in the circle of light. "I never was much for talk. Always believed that half the trouble in the world came from open mouths. But I would have talked to you about this, Nick."

"No, you wouldn't have. You wouldn't believe me when I told you the truth."

He sat there with the folded newspaper in his lap,

not frowning now, but pursing his lips and looking at the ceiling. Finally he said, "It's a pretty hard thing to believe, Nick."

"I can't help that," I said.

He stared at me. "You mean to tell me that wasn't you who broke those church windows?"

"It wasn't me. I swear on the Bible. I was up at the Daubers' the whole time. Mrs. Dauber and Gypsy were playing hearts when I got there, and then me and Gypsy went out to feed the chickens and talk for a while."

"Can you see how hard it is for me—for all of us—to believe that?"

"Yes," I said. "I can see that. But it wasn't me."

He put the newspaper down on the sofa, stood up, and came over to where I was standing by the door. He put his hand on my shoulder. I could tell it wasn't an easy thing for him to do. "All right, Nick. I believe you. You can quit working at the church. I'll work it out with Clampett."

I didn't want to be forgiven for something I hadn't done. Let them suffer for it. It was a funny way to feel, for I was the one who was suffering, but that was the way I felt. "No, I want to finish the job. There isn't much left anyway."

He took his hand off my shoulder and considered for a minute. "Okay," he said. "But you don't have to do it."

"I want to."

He paused. "Let's hope something like this doesn't happen again."

"If it does," I said, "it won't be me the next time, either." The minute the words were out of my mouth, I was sorry I'd said them.

He gave me a quick, sharp look. "Nick, there'd better be no next time." I knew he was wondering if he had been wrong to believe me, wondering if maybe my troublesomeness had grown into something worse—something that nobody would want to think about.

On Sunday afternoon I went on up to the graveyard. There really wasn't much more to do—five or six more graves to trim, a couple of paths to weed and rake. I collected my tools from the church basement and went out to the graveyard, then through it toward the back where it ended at the stone wall. I was coming along to the graves I had yet to do when my eye caught something out of order up ahead. Something pretty big was lying flat on the ground. I stood still, feeling a little spooked. I didn't really want to go over and see what it was, but I knew I had to. I took a tight grip on the sickle, just in case, and went on over.

A gravestone had fallen over. That surprised me, for the back end of the graveyard was the last to be used—some of the graves there were only a year old. I would expect the old stones at the front to tip from age. I'd straightened up a couple of small ones. But these newer stones wouldn't fall over by themselves.

It wasn't just the stone, either. The turf over the grave was all tossed around—dirt, clumps of grass, stones as big as potatoes showing. I stood there staring. An animal could have dug up the turf like that. Skunks will dig, looking for beetles and such. But a skunk wouldn't have flung up big stones. A woodchuck, maybe, or a dog smelling something down in the dirt. But not likely.

But no woodchuck or dog had knocked over that gravestone. I crouched over the stone. It had fallen forward, so the writing was facedown. I knew I had to get it back up, for I was certain to be blamed for knocking it down. Besides, I was mighty curious to see who was buried there.

I knelt in front of it, grabbed underneath it, and

heaved. I could raise the stone a few inches, but then I had to change my grip around to get under it, and I couldn't. I dropped the stone with a thump and stood. Now what? Maybe I could find a branch out in the woods to use as a pry bar. I walked in that direction until I came to the stone wall. A better idea came to me. I took a stone about the size of a small pumpkin off the wall, wrapped my arms around it to hold it against my belly, toted it back, and laid it by the gravestone. I knelt again and heaved the gravestone up until I'd gotten it ten inches off the ground. With my knee I pushed the rock under the gravestone and let the gravestone rest on it.

Now I could get some leverage. I stood and heaved, grunting and sweating. When I'd got it to about a forty-five-degree angle, I got my back under it and heaved it up the rest of the way. I tamped the ground around it to hold it in place. Then I raked the dirt smooth. Anyone who took a look in daylight would believe that some animal had been at it, nothing else.

I knelt in front of the gravestone. Because the stone was pretty new, I had no trouble reading the words. They said:

JARED SOLTERS

JULY 18, 1905 – OCTOBER 24, 1918

HE DIED AMONG STRANGERS

I stood there, staring at the writing. He'd died right at the time the epidemic was at its worst in Stoneybeach. He was my age when he died— thirteen. I stood there calculating. Almost exactly my age, when you got down to it, minus a couple of weeks. What surprised me was the words they'd put on the gravestone: HE DIED AMONG STRANGERS. Why would they have put that? Why hadn't they put something more regular, the kind of writing that was on most of the stones—GONE TO HIS HEAVENLY REST, MAY HE REST IN PEACE, that kind of thing?

I sure wanted to know more about him, this Jared Solters. Wanted to know about him really bad. Was there a way to find out? Did they have a list of the ones who died at the village hall? I could ask Mrs. Bettencamp, the town clerk. She'd know where there was some information. Maybe over at Millbury.

I bent over, picked up the rock I'd used to raise the gravestone, wrapped my arms around it again, and toted it back to the stone wall. As I was setting it in place, I saw something out of the corner of my eye—just a motion, nothing I could make out. I swung my head. Somebody or something was crouching in the shadows of the hardwood stand, half hidden behind the trunk of a big oak. I couldn't make out anything about him—her, it—except that it was small. A little woman, maybe. Or a kid. I started to climb up on the stone wall to get a better look. It vanished in the shadows so quick I didn't see it move. Just disappeared in a finger snap. "Hey," I shouted. There was no answer. I turned, collected my tools, and got on out of there.

Chapter Four

Who was it? Or what? I had trouble going to sleep that night, and trouble staying asleep, too. I'd wake up, my heart pounding. Then I'd make myself think about something nice—going for a movie and ice cream sodas over to Millbury, the Labor Day picnic, with plenty of corn and a softball game. I'd doze off for a while, and then wake up, my heart pounding again.

Finally it got to be daylight, which was a relief. I got dressed, went down early, and got the coffee going. After awhile Uncle Jack came down. "You're up early," he said. "It's not like you."

"Didn't sleep too good," I said. "Felt like getting up."

"Oh?" he said.

But before he could ask what was bothering me, I jumped in. "I guess it's okay if I visit Gypsy?"

He got down the frying pan and put some strips of bacon in it. "I don't guess it would do any good to say no, would it?"

"She's my best friend. It's too much to ask me not to see her." That was another one of my expressions: it's too much to ask.

"How come she's your best friend? What's the matter with some of the other kids? Joey Pileski, for example. Nice, decent boy, always got his socks pulled up and shirttail in, not like some I know."

"I could mention a couple of things about Joey Pileski," I said.

"Oh?"

"He's not as decent as the grown-ups think."

"Well, you could have fooled me."

"He did fool you. He's got all the grown-ups fooled. He doesn't fool the kids."

"Beats Gypsy Dauber, I should think," he said, turning over the bacon with a fork. "She's troublesome. That's why you like her. All the Daubers are troublesome. The old man hasn't drawn a sober breath since before the war, and Mrs. Dauber steals.

That's what they say."

I looked at him. "You're always the first one to tell me not to put any stock in what people say." I figured Mrs. Dauber did steal, but I wasn't about to say so.

He pulled at his chin. "Well, you're right there, Nick. I don't know that for sure. But it isn't any rumor that old man Dauber drinks."

I wanted to get off the subject of the Daubers. I had more important things to talk about. "Uncle Jack, how come nobody ever talks about the flu epidemic?"

He turned away from the stove to give me a look. "What put that in your mind all of a sudden?"

"Mrs. Dauber said something about it the other day. How her cousin had died from it." Mrs. Dauber didn't have any cousins that I'd ever heard of.

"It's best to leave it alone, Nick. It's over and done with a long time ago."

"I have a right to know, Uncle Jack, seeing as my ma and pa died in it."

He took two plates down from the shelf, divided the bacon onto them, and broke a couple of eggs into the hot bacon fat. The smell of eggs and bacon, along with the coffee, was mighty fine. I waited. Finally he said, "You got to remember, I was in France during most of it. Pretty bad over there, too. Lost a lot of fellas to it. But a soldier didn't have any choice about it. Couldn't run away from the flu any more than you could run away from German machine guns. Over here people had choices, and I guess some made bad ones. A lot of people made bad choices, I reckon."

"I don't get you, Uncle Jack."

He spooned some hot fat over the eggs so the yolk would cook through. "It was right bad, the flu. Your lungs filled up and you began to drown in it. Most people got better—four out of five, something like that. But a lot didn't. Sometimes it'd kill you in four days. Soldier I heard of in Camp Devens was walking along and just dropped down dead. There were dead everywhere. The problem was, nobody wanted to touch them. Some people wouldn't tend their own—wouldn't go into a room where their own children, wife, husband, sister, was dying. Just let them die by themselves. Not everybody—a lot of people took their chances to care for others, and some of them caught the flu and died, too. But there were ones that didn't. A lot of them. Like I say, I didn't see much of it in Stoneybeach because I was overseas until that October. I came home to find my brother and his wife dead and buried. The stories were still fresh in people's minds. Some of them were angry and disgusted about some friend or relative who'd been neglected by a wife or husband. I heard some things. Enough to get an idea of it. I guess that's why you don't hear much talk about it. Too many things weren't done the way they should have been done, and people wanted to put it out of their minds. Some were worse than others, but I guess everybody was left with something on their conscience. Everybody wanted to forget about it."

"Was that what happened to Ma and Pa? Nobody took care of them?" I hated the idea of that.

"I couldn't rightly say. I wasn't here, Nick, and nobody would have told me they were neglected if it had been the case. Most likely they were beyond saving anyway." He slipped a big spoon under the eggs and slid them onto the plates. "Keep it in mind that a lot of people did everything they could for the sick ones. But I reckon there weren't too many saints around. Saints went out of style a long while back." He looked at me. "People aren't going to be grateful to you for bringing it up." He carried the plates to the table. "Eat up," he said. "We're getting late for work with all this palavering."

That evening after supper I went out to Gypsy's. Twilight was coming. I'd hardly gotten off the road into their yard when I wished I hadn't come. Mr. Dauber was passed out in the weeds by the house, holding a near-empty whiskey bottle by the neck and snoring as loud as a steam whistle. I skirted around him and went into the house. Nobody was there. Where was Gypsy? Suddenly I got the thought that the old man had hit her with something and killed her. I looked into her bedroom, which was off the kitchen. Bed unmade as usual, but nobody there. No sign of Mrs. Dauber, either.

I went out the kitchen door into the barnyard. The chickens hadn't been housed up yet and were still clucking around the barnyard waiting for a fox to get them. "Where's Gypsy, you fools?" She must have heard me, for she came out of the shadows of the barn. In the twilight I couldn't see her too well, but I could see well enough to know she was crying. Her hands were balled up by her sides, and one of her cheeks was red and swelled up. "Someday I'm going to kill him, I swear I will."

"What'd he hit you with?"

"The skillet," she said. She gasped out a big sob. "I'll kill him, I swear it. He was raging around the house because there wasn't no supper for him. We already ate. How was we supposed to know he was coming home? He ain't been home for three days. He shouted at Ma to fry him up some ham and potatoes. She told him we didn't have no ham. He snatched down the skillet and took a swing at her, but being drunk he missed and fell down. She ran off to Old Man Sneakers's to borrow a piece of ham. Falling down like that made him madder than ever. He shouted at me to fry some potatoes. I said I couldn't, being as he had the skillet. He shouted, 'I'll learn you to answer back,' and before I could duck, he whanged me with the skillet." She snapped her fists by her sides again. "I'm going to kill him someday."

I felt bad for her. I didn't know what to say. I never could think of the right thing in such cases. The best thing I could come up with was "You ought to put some cold water on that swelling."

She touched the swelling. "The heck with it. I don't care."

Talking to me had calmed her down some. "Maybe we ought to go someplace until he sobers up," I said.

"Naw. He won't stir until sunup. He'll feel sick as a dog and hang his head down and tell me and Ma he's sorry, he won't never do it again, he's sworn off liquor, and this time he means it. And he *will* mean it. He'll make us clean up on Sunday and go to church, and by about Wednesday he'll get to where he can't stand being good no more and go off to Millbury and get tanked up again, the way he always does."

"Listen, Gypsy, we better get the chickens in. It won't help any if the foxes get them."

She rubbed her eyes to get the tears out. "Okay," she said. So we started herding them into the henhouse. When we got them locked up for the night, and she was a little more normal, I said, "I got something to tell you, Gypsy. I saw him—it. Whatever it is."

It was too big a change of subject for her. "Who?"

"Whatever it is that's getting me in trouble."

"You saw it?"

"Yeah. In the stand of hardwood behind the cemetery."

"I told you it was a wood spirit."

We went around behind the barn and sat side by side, looking at the last red light from the sun fading out on the piney hills. "I don't think it's any wood spirits," I said. "I can't figure out what it is. See, there's more to it. What happened was, I noticed this headstone at the back of the cemetery, near the stone wall. It was tipped over and the ground over the grave was all messed up. I got the gravestone pushed back up and tamped the ground down so it wouldn't fall over again. That's when I saw whatever it was, crouched down in the shadows maybe a couple of hundred feet into the woods. Couldn't make it out. Then I moved and it disappeared. Gone, just like that."

She'd gotten interested. "You couldn't see nothing about it?"

"Just a shape. Just a movement."

"You figure it come into the cemetery and knocked over that gravestone?"

"Must have. It knew I was working out there and would get blamed for anything that went wrong. Just happened I saw it before anyone else did." I paused: here was the part I didn't much like to think about. "That gravestone. It was for a kid named Jared Solters. Died during the flu epidemic." I turned to look at her. "Almost exactly the same age as I am right now, short a couple of weeks."

She looked back at me. "What do you make of that, Nick? Why'd he choose that gravestone?"

I didn't say anything for a minute. "Maybe it was just by chance."

"I don't believe it was just by chance. Do you?"

"I got my doubts," I said.

We were quiet for a while, looking at the last tinge of red fade out on the pines. Then she said, "What're you going to do, Nick?"

"I figure I got to catch this—whatever it is. There's no two ways about it. He's determined to get me in trouble. He isn't picking on anyone else, just me. I don't know why. Can't think of any reason for it. But he's after me, and someday he's going to get me into real trouble. Serious trouble. What if he sets a house afire? What if he kills somebody, Gypsy?"

She lightly rubbed her cheek where her pa had bruised it. "You think he might do that, Nick?"

"I don't know. I'm scared he might. If he kills someone, I might get the electric chair."

"Would they really do that to you?" She looked at me kind of awed that she knew someone who might get the electric chair.

"I don't know, Gypsy. If he started burning down

houses and killing people, they'd have to, wouldn't they? They might not even bother to call the police about it. They might just come to the house at night, grab me out of bed, and hang me from a tree, the way they did to cattle rustlers out west. Never bothered to give them a trial, just took them out and hung them from a tree."

"Wouldn't your uncle Jack stop them?"

"What could he do?" I said.

"You got to catch him, Nick. You just have to."

But how? It was near dark now. "I've got to go," I said. "You sure you're okay?"

"Pa won't stir until sunup. I'll slide my bureau in front of my bedroom door. But he won't stir."

I went on home.

How was I going to catch it, whatever it was that was pretending to be me? That night in bed I turned it over and over in my mind. I had to find out more about this Jared Solters. I didn't know where it would lead, but it would be a start.

I decided not to say anything about it to Uncle Jack. He'd be against it, against raising dust when there wasn't any need for it, he'd say. I didn't think he'd try to stop me from investigating it, but he might. No use taking a chance.

A couple of days later Uncle Jack sent me to the post office to pick up a package of brass fittings he'd ordered. The post office was in Ben Schmidt's general store. Two doors over were the village offices, upstairs over the firehouse. I went on up there. Not much to see: tax assessor's office, village clerk's office, meeting room for the village selectmen. The door to the village clerk's office was always open, and I went in. Filing cabinets, a couple of desks, a map of the village on the wall. The village clerk, Mrs. Bettencamp, sat behind a desk. Dark blue blouse, gray hair pulled back. "Hello, Mrs. Bettencamp," I said.

"Hello, Nick. What can I do for you?"

I wasn't sure what I wanted. "I was wondering, do you have files of old newspapers and stuff?"

"No, we don't keep things like that. Don't have the space. You'd have to go over to the *Gazette* office in Millbury."

"Oh," I said. "What other things do you have? I mean, records of people."

She looked at me a little sideways. I could see that the word was going around about me being up to something. "What exactly are you looking for, Nick?"

I didn't want to tell her much, but I had to tell her something. "I wanted to look up people who died in the flu epidemic."

"Oh, Nick," she said. "Why go into all that? It's over and done with. There's no way we can bring those people back."

"My folks died in it. I just want to find out more about it. There's nothing wrong with that, is there?"

She gave me a suspicious look. "I don't see the good of it, but you'll find the vital records for Stoneybeach in those ledgers on that shelf there."

"Vital records?"

"Births and deaths. It's from the Latin word for life."

"Oh." I said *vital records* under my breath a couple of times to pin it down. It might be a good expression to have.

The ledgers had thick, stiff covers and were a good deal taller than ordinary books. They were set out by years. I took down the one that had 1918 in it. It was just page after page of births and deaths, line after line, written by somebody with good, clear handwriting. I ran a finger down the line until I saw my ma and pa in there, died two days apart.

A little farther along I came to Jared Solters, died October 24. Nothing more about him than that: born and died.

Next I ran my finger up and down the line through the whole of that time when the flu epidemic struck Stoneybeach, from September into November. No sign of any other Solters. What happened to his family? Weren't from Stoneybeach, that was clear. If they were, they'd have buried Jared themselves and would have put something else besides DIED AMONG STRANGERS on his gravestone—something like SNATCHED AWAY UNTIMELY because he was young, or GONE TO A BETTER PLACE if they were religious.

I put the ledger back on the shelf and went over to Mrs. Bettencamp. "Is there any way to find out more about somebody who died?"

"Nick, if you're so interested in your family, why not ask Jack?"

Of course it wasn't my family I was looking for. "He doesn't like to talk about the epidemic and all that," I said.

She gave me a stern look. "Most folks don't. They'd just as soon leave it lie. And I'd advise you to do the same."

I knew I ought to keep on the good side of as many people as I could. "I guess you're right, Mrs. Bettencamp." I turned as if I were going, but then at the door I stopped. "Did you ever hear of a family around here called Solters?"

"Solters? Is that who you were looking up?"

"No," I said. "Somebody told me that my pa had a friend called Mr. Solters. I figured he might be able to tell me about Pa."

Mrs. Bettencamp shook her head. "Not around Stoneybeach, Nick. Might have been some fella who worked on the fishing boats for awhile, but I don't recall any family by that name being in residence. Not in my time, anyway."

Being in residence. That was a good expression. So was *not in my time.* Mrs. Bettencamp was sure a good one for expressions. Maybe that was why they'd made her village clerk. "Well, I should probably forget it, I guess," I said. "Thanks." And I left.

It was a mystery, all right. How come this kid died here if he didn't have any family around? Who paid for his gravestone? Would the *Millbury Gazette* have written a story about it? If there'd been some mystery about it, they might have. I'd have to go over to Millbury to find out. Uncle Jack had to go over there from time to time to pick up marine hardware and stuff that came by Railway Express. But if I asked to ride over with him, he'd want to know why. How was I going to do it?

On Sunday afternoon I told Uncle Jack I was going to visit Gypsy. But instead I went out to the church and went through the graveyard back to where that kid was buried. I took a careful look around. The stone was standing up the way it was supposed to, but the grass and dirt over the grave looked to me like it had been scuffed a little. Not much; maybe some, as if somebody had been doing something there.

It was a pretty day: blue sky, sun beaming down, a little breeze coming off the bay to keep it from getting too hot. I walked over to the stone wall at the back of the cemetery and looked out into the stand of hardwoods, glancing carefully here and there among the oaks and maples. Nothing to see except the birds, squirrels, chipmunks, and such.

I climbed over the stone wall and walked through the hardwood stand toward the piney hills, going slow and easy, trying not to make too much noise. I kept moving my head from side to side. Every fifty feet I stopped dead to listen. Then I would move on again.

It took me fifteen minutes to get through the hardwood stand to the point where the land began to slant upward into the hills and the pine forest began. Here I stopped again. Long, narrow sunbeams slanted down through the pines. Motes of dust floated in the sunbeams. Everything else was shadowy. He—it—had to be up in the pine forest somewhere. If he'd been hanging around the village, people would have spotted him. I shivered. Didn't want to meet up with him, that was for sure. But I didn't see where I had any choice. I had to talk to him. Of course he might be a kind of creature that didn't talk. Ghosts didn't talk, so far as I knew, if there was any such thing as ghosts. Gypsy said there was—had seen one float across the barn roof one moonlit night. Uncle Jack said there wasn't. I didn't think there was, either, but I couldn't vouch for it. Might be, after all.

So there was no telling whether this creature, this other me out there, could talk. I took a deep breath and began moving on again. In some cases the lower of the pine branches had died, the way they do, and I could see through them a fair distance. But where the lower pine branches were still alive and covered with needles, they blocked off the view—stood right in my face like a curtain, and I had to push through them without knowing what was beyond.

I was now maybe a couple of hundred yards in the pine forest. The ground was rising steeply and my legs were beginning to feel it. I stopped and listened. Nothing but the light breathing of the breeze among the pine branches. I moved forward again and suddenly saw a dark shape among the shadows of the tree trunks. My heart jumped. I knew right away it wasn't natural, for the lines of the shape, as much as I could make out, anyway, were straight, not curved or twisted the way they'd be if it was a piece of ledge or a fallen tree.

I dropped flat onto the soft pine needles, the smell of them bright in my nose. My breath was coming fast. What if he were some kind of ghost you could put your hand through? What if he could drill holes into you with his eyes, or melt your skin with his breath? What if he were just plain dead—dead with no life inside him, no feelings about things, cold as ice when you touched him, but mad because he was dead and wanted to kill somebody else to get even? I shivered again, and for a minute I thought about sliding back the way I'd come and hightailing it for home.

But I knew I couldn't. I started pulling myself along over the slippery pine needles. When I'd gone twenty feet, I stopped and stared ahead again. I could see the shape pretty clear now—some kind of little hut or something, just about big enough for a kid to sleep in.

I started sliding forward again, and soon I could see the details. Built out of scrap lumber. You could find stuff like that in people's backyards, or behind shops—parts of a packing case, an old door, a window sash from a henhouse, a piece of two-by-four. A blanket hung up for a door, and a window was built into one end. It was the kind of hut that kids were always building out in the woods. Wouldn't be any good in the winter, but it'd do fine in warm weather.

Was he there? Might be out looking for dinner. Of course maybe he was the kind of thing that didn't have to eat. I took a deep breath and began sliding forward again. Soon I was close enough to the hut to touch it. My heart was racing and sweat was cold on my face. Slowly I rose up on my knees and peered in through the window.

He was lying on his side on an old brown army blanket, his eyes closed. His head was resting on one arm so I could see his face plain enough. It was my face—the same face I used to see in the mirror every morning. I froze dead still, and the queerest feeling came over me. I was looking at myself. Same brown hair not quite combed right, same nose, same lips, same everything. He was wearing the same shirt and pants I had on, the same shoes. There was something funny about the shirt, though, and it took me a little bit to figure it out. It was buttoned the wrong way, right side over left, the way girls' shirts and jackets are made. I looked at his hair. It was parted opposite to mine, too. Without thinking, I raised my hand to my shirt buttons to make sure I was right. In an instant he sat up and stared out the window. For a minute we were eye to eye, our faces hardly two feet apart, like we were each looking in a mirror. Then he flung himself through the blanket door. I dove for him and caught him by one leg. He stumbled and fell. "Hold still," I cried. He grunted, and with his free leg kicked me hard on the side of the head. I went dizzy and he went crashing off through the pine branches, going upward into the hills. I knelt up, staring dizzily after him. There was no use chasing him, for he'd lose me in the thick pine forest in a minute.

Chapter Five

When I got home, Uncle Jack wasn't there. He'd left a note that he'd gone over to help Miss Bell with her accounts, and that I was to get my own supper. I was just as glad to be alone, for I had an awful lot to think about. I heated up a can of baked beans, sliced off a couple of chunks of pumpernickel, and sat down to think about everything while I ate my supper.

He—it—whichever it was—wasn't any ghost. He was solid, all right. My head was still sore from where he'd kicked me. That was one thing. For another, he was identical to me. An *other* me. Only backward, like a mirror reflection. That much I knew for a fact.

But who was he? Was he me? Did he think like me? Did he have the same feelings as me? Or were his thoughts and feelings backward to mine? It gave me the strangest sort of feeling to know that there was this other me out there. That someone had stolen my *me.*

What right had he to do that? I was *me*, not him. The whole thing was weird. It was making me feel like nothing around me was real anymore. Like I might start walking through walls, flying through the air.

I had to talk to somebody, so I washed up my plate and things and went out to Gypsy's. We sat behind the barn watching the sun go down, and I told Gypsy the whole thing—slipping up through the pine forest, seeing him face to face like a reflection, catching him by the leg, and getting kicked in the head for it.

"He's hard, like a person?" she said.

"Yeah, he's real—at least to hang on to." I shook my head. "I can't figure out what I did to him that's got him so mad at me."

"What's it feel like, Nick?" She was mighty curious about how people felt. "I mean, having this other one around."

"Weird. It feels weird. It's making me crazy. I'm beginning to lose track of who I am myself. Maybe it's my punishment for being troublesome. Or not having parents or something. Or both. They're sort of mixed up in my mind. I can understand why I ought to be punished for being troublesome, but why should I be punished for not having parents? I wish I hadn't been troublesome. I wish I was more good. I wish I'd studied more, instead of reading Oz books. I wish I'd got on the good side of Miss Quince, the way Joey Pileski does."

"Joey Pileski ain't so hot. He doesn't get caught is all."

I looked at her. "Don't you ever want to be good? Study and get good grades?"

"Naw," she said. "I like being this way. I'm gonna drop out of school as soon as I can."

"And do what?"

"Go over to Millbury and get a job in the paper mills. Make myself some dough. You can make twenty-five dollars a week in the paper mill, Pa says. He says he would do it, but he don't like being beholden to nobody."

According to Uncle Jack, Mr. Dauber drank himself out of every good job he ever had, but I didn't say that. Instead I said, "The thing is, if I'd always been good, like Joey—"

"They only think he's good."

"—the way people think, people wouldn't have been so quick to blame me for what this other me is doing."

"What're you going to do, Nick?"

I shook my head. "I don't know. I've got to catch him. Got to talk to him, anyway."

"How're you gonna do that?"

"I don't know. But I've got to figure out something. Lay a trap for him."

"What're you gonna bait him with?"

"Me. I've got to bait him with myself."

"With yourself? Nick, you can't trust him. Maybe he'll get some kind of magical power over you."

I'd thought about that, too. "That's what worries me. Worries me a lot. I wish I knew what his plan is. It might be that he's just trying to get me in trouble for some reason I don't understand. It might be that he's trying to take me over, the whole me. He's got my looks, my body already. What if he goes after my mind? My feelings and all. Gets into my head somehow and starts changing everything around. Taking things out, putting his things in.

Where'd I be then?" I shivered and rubbed my hands together.

"Could he do that?"

"I don't know," I said. "I don't know anything."

"Do you think he's trying to kill you?"

I shrugged. "Maybe. If he could figure out a way to do it. That'd clear the field for him. He could move in with Uncle Jack, take over my room and all."

She was looking pretty scared. "Nick, what if he has a knife when you bait him?"

I shrugged. "I've got to chance it. Sooner or later he's going to do something real bad, and the whole town'll come after me."

My thoughts were coming and going pretty fast as I walked home. I felt stuck, surrounded by wild things that were circling around me, waving their arms, snarling and snapping their jaws, so there was no way for me to get out. "Why me? What did I do?" I said aloud. But there was no answer.

I was glad to see the lights of our house, for it'd feel safe in there. I walked in. Uncle Jack and Miss Bell were at the parlor with the little table between them. The cribbage cards were laid out between them, but they weren't playing. When I walked in, they stopped dead and stared at me. "What?" I said.

Uncle Jack said softly, "What was that all about, Nick?"

I looked straight back at them. "What all about?" But I knew.

"What you did twenty minutes ago. Walked in here looking wild and cursing like we weren't here. Went up to your room and slammed the door." He stared at me. "Don't you even remember?"

Nothing I said would be right. If I said I remembered, I'd be guilty of it, and if I said I didn't remember, they'd think I was crazy. I tried to make my voice steady. "It wasn't me. I was out at Gypsy's."

But of course it was no use. "You weren't out at Gypsy's, Nick. You were right here. I don't know how you got away. I went up to your room. Your clothes were flung all over the place, the chair was tipped over, and you were gone. Got out by the window somehow, I reckoned."

I didn't say anything. There was nothing to say. Miss Bell looked at Uncle Jack. "He's having a mental disturbance, Jack. He needs to see a doctor."

They were talking around me. There wasn't any point in standing there. I walked out of the parlor and went on upstairs to see what the other me had done. Messed up my room for certain—pants and shirts flung on the floor, Oz books pushed in a heap off the bureau onto the floor, pictures of the goat and the fat lady hanging sideways.

The window was open and the breeze was blowing in. I stuck my head out. It was a tough climb down out of there, but there was a way to do it—for I'd done it before. He'd have had to grab hold of the gutter along the roof above the window and rest his feet on the top trim of the kitchen window below. Then he could have jumped across to the roof of the kitchen stoop and shinnied down the roof post. He could do it, but he would have had to know how. Did he get that out of my brain? I went cold, closed the window, and began straightening things up.

How'd he know I wasn't home? He must have spied on the house. When he'd seen me leave, he'd followed me up to Gypsy's, waited until he saw me settle in behind the barn, and then come on back here. Something like that, anyway. It didn't much matter, really.

The next morning Uncle Jack didn't say anything about it. In fact, he hardly said anything at all. But he was watching me real close, and when we got to the boatyard, he set me to scraping the hull of a sail-boat we were to paint, where he could keep a close eye on me. Just watching, giving me a quick glance every few minutes.

It went on like that for two or three days, and when I hadn't done anything strange, he began to relax a little bit, although he kept me around the boatyard—didn't send me off on errands or any-thing. I had sense enough not to go out to Gypsy's in the evening, either. I didn't want to give the other me another chance to come in and wreck the house.

Then one morning the fire alarm blew. Nothing unusual about that: we had a fire alarm once or twice a week. It usually wasn't anything—some-body left something burning on the stove or set a field on fire burning rubbish. A lot of the men in town belonged to the volunteer fire company and went to fires. Uncle Jack had belonged for awhile, but he wasn't much of a joiner and had dropped out.

Uncle Jack listened to the alarm for a minute. You could tell from the number of whistles where the fire was. "Over by the school," he said. We waited, and then came the wail of the siren rising up and down. Uncle Jack shrugged, and we went back to work. But I wasn't feeling any too good about it—mighty uneasy, no two ways about it. By and by there came the "fire out" signal. I wanted to know in the worst way what it was, but I kept on working, and about ten minutes later Constable Ace Tumulty drove into the yard in his police Chevy. He was the only cop we had in town—couldn't afford any more and didn't need more than one anyway, Uncle Jack said. Mostly he directed traffic when there was a village meeting, went to fires, broke up fights when some fishermen got tanked up. Constable Tumulty was an older man with white hair, but he was beefy and could still handle a couple of drunk fishermen.

"Hello, Ace," Uncle Jack said. "What was it?"

"School," he said. He frowned and took a quick look at me.

I felt cold and sick to my stomach. I didn't say anything—nothing to say.

"The school? Much damage?"

"No. We caught her in time. Good thing, too. Old wooden building like that would've went up in fifteen minutes. Only reason we got there soon enough was that Widow Clarke saw it set. She was standin' by her window in the kitchen across the way, throwin' bread crumbs to the birdies like she does. She seen this boy come around the back corner of the school with an armload of papers and a bucket. He crumpled them papers against the corner of the school building, right there near the cellar door. Splashed something from the bucket around, tossed a match. It flared up. As soon as he seen that the wood was flaming, he ran for it. Went right by her kitchen window, stopped there to look back and see if the fire was burning good. He wasn't but ten feet away from her—she showed me where he stood. He stayed there looking at the fire four or five seconds, and then took off again." He looked at me and back at Uncle Jack. "It was Nick."

The other me had figured it all out. Set the fire in broad daylight, then stopped by Widow Clarke's window so she'd get a good look at him. Did it all on purpose. I felt sick and trapped—and angry. What did he have against me? I looked at Uncle Jack. "Uncle Jack, I—"

Uncle Jack didn't pay any attention to me. "Ace, it wasn't Nick. I know that for a fact. He's been here the whole morning since we opened up at eight. Hasn't been out of my sight for more'n five minutes at a stretch, much less enough time to col-lect paper and a bucket of kerosene and get over to the school and back. Not a chance of it. It wasn't Nick."

Then he turned and looked at me, head cocked, one eye shut, like he was seeing me in a new way. "What do you make of it, Nick?"

But before I could say anything, Constable Tumulty said, "Jack, I know you feel real bad about this. You raised Nick since he wasn't nothing but a baby and can't help feelin' for the boy. But Widow Clarke, she was standin' by her window, throwin' bread crumbs to the birdies and seen the whole thing. Nick wasn't ten feet from her. She seen him plain as day—couldn't miss."

"Ace, you ever know me to lie?" Uncle Jack said.

"No, I can't say as I have, Jack. But there's always a first time. Wouldn't blame you, most likely do the same thing myself if I was in your shoes. But she seen him."

"It wasn't him. He's been in my sight the entire morning. What time she say it was?"

"Just after ten. She knew, because she always feeds them birdies around ten, and she looked at the clock. I guess she figures they'll get sore at her if she don't come through on time."

"I'll swear in court that Nick was here with me the whole time."

Constable Tumulty frowned and stared down at the ground for a minute. Then he said, "Jack, we all know that Nick gets troublesome at times. Not a bad boy, nobody's said that, but troublesome now and again. And from what I hear, it's been getting worse lately. It ain't something we can let pass." The constable looked at me. "Nick, I know your uncle Jack is tryin' to help you, but it won't do no good. Best all around for you to confess, so Jack don't get hisself into trouble coverin' up for you."

There wasn't any use telling him about the other me. He'd just laugh. "It wasn't me, Constable Tumulty. I don't care what Widow Clarke says. I was here the whole morning, like Uncle Jack says."

Constable Tumulty shook his head. "I just wish you two wouldn't be so all-fired stubborn about it. Breaking a couple of windows in the church was one thing—wasn't the first time a kid flung stones through a window. But it's gettin' dangerous. We can't have it no more. Settin' fire to a building ain't no prank. Suppose somebody was in there? We can't take a chance on what the boy's going to do next."

Uncle Jack shook his head. "Ace, you know what you know, and I know what I know. This boy's been under my eye all morning. He didn't set that school afire any more than the man in the moon did."

Constable Tumulty looked grim, his mouth tight, his hands on his hips. "Jack, we ain't just got a witness. We got the bucket he flung down. I got five people who'll swear it smelled of kerosene when we come across it. I'm taking it over to the state police barracks in Millbury. They'll go over it for fingerprints. I'm pretty confident what they'll find."

He left. We went into the boatyard shop. What kind of fingerprints were they going to find? Would the other me have fingerprints? Would they be the same as mine?

Uncle Jack went behind the counter and sat on the stool there. "What's it all about, Nick?"

"There's somebody out there who looks like me. I don't mean a little like me, or even a lot like me. He looks exactly like me."

He stared at me. "You sure of this? You've seen this boy?"

"Yes. I saw him. He built himself a little cabin up

98

there in the pines behind the cemetery. I noticed him out there and tracked him back into the forest. Got close enough to tackle him, but he broke loose and got away."

"You laid hands on him?"

"Yes."

"Why didn't you tell me about this kid before?"

"You wouldn't have believed me. You wouldn't believe me when I said I didn't throw stones at the church or curse at you and mess up my room."

He thought for a minute. "I guess not." He looked at me, watching my face real close. "What do you make of it?"

"I don't know what to make of it, Uncle Jack. I don't know where he came from or anything. I don't know why he's doing what he's doing. But it was him who came into the house the other night and tore up my room. It was him who broke those windows in the church."

He went on staring at me real close, trying to make up his mind. Finally he said, "You can understand why people have a hard time believing you, Nick."

"Yes, I can. Sometimes I have a hard time believing it myself. Sometimes I feel like I must be going crazy."

When he heard that, his face kind of softened down. "To be honest, Nick, I was beginning to think you were going crazy myself. Disturbed. Whatever they call it when it's a kid. And if it weren't for today I probably would have. But I *know* where you were when that fire was set. So I can believe that there's some troublesome kid who happens to look a lot like you around. Some runaway kid living rough and stealing whatever he can for a living. Just hard luck on you that he's got a resemblance to you."

Finally he believed me. That was the most relieved I'd ever felt. Just the idea that somebody believed me almost made me want to cry. It wasn't just having somebody on my side—it was being believed. Of course Gypsy believed me, but she'd believe most anything. Uncle Jack, he was realistic—had seen too much in his life to be any way else. And he believed me.

But it wasn't just hard luck that the other me looked like me. He'd picked me deliberate. I couldn't say that, though—not yet, anyway. "Uncle Jack, it isn't just a close resemblance. I saw him up close. We're identical."

"Nick, I just don't see how that can be. Close

resemblance, sure. That happens. We all take some-body for somebody else sometimes when we get only a quick look. But I'll bet if the two of you were to stand side by side, everybody would see the dif-ference between you plain enough."

"You wouldn't. There isn't any difference. Except this: he's got his shirt buttoned the wrong way across. Right over left instead of left over right."

Uncle Jack shrugged. "That doesn't mean very much. Living rough, picking up stuff out of garbage bins, stealing like as not, he could have found a woman's shirt somewhere, put it on for lack of any-thing better."

I decided not to push it. I was glad enough to have Uncle Jack believe me and didn't want to raise a lot of questions. "I guess so," I said.

"Now listen, Nick, I want you to stop worrying about it. Ace Tumulty's going to get the fingerprints off that bucket and that'll settle it." Then he con-sidered. "You haven't been fooling around with a bucket like that somewhere, have you?"

I thought about it. "Not that I remember. Not recently, anyway." I'd forgotten about the finger-prints, and now I started to get nervous all over again. "Uncle Jack, what if he's got the same fingerprints as me, like he's got my hair, my eyes, and such?"

He smiled, stood, walked around the counter to where I was standing, and put his arm around my shoulder. "That can't happen, Nick. Don't let it worry you. We'll have this all straightened out pretty soon."

But I knew that Uncle Jack was wrong; it wasn't going to be straightened out all that soon.

Chapter Six

It's funny how you can get used to things.

I'd gotten used to standing away from store windows and such when I was with anybody. Automatically stood back a ways, or off at an angle. Didn't have to think about it much. Still, I had to do something pretty quick. He was closing in on me. There was no telling how this fingerprint stuff would come out.

I didn't have long to wait. That afternoon Constable Tumulty came over to the boatyard, collected me, and drove me over to the state police barracks in Millbury. Eleven miles. I was pretty tense and nerved up—couldn't get myself relaxed. Tried breathing deep, tried humming, tried thinking of ice cream and cake. Nothing worked.

The fingerprinting didn't take five minutes. They pressed my fingers one at a time onto an ink pad and rolled each fingertip into a space on a card. They gave me some mineral spirits to clean my hands with, and we left.

Once we were outside I said, "Constable Tumulty, I've got to look something up in the library here before I go home."

He gave me a long look. "I don't like to leave you wanderin' around on your own. I told Jack I'd see you safe home. Maybe better do it another time."

"I don't get much chance to come over to Millbury," I said. "It's about my ma and pa dying in the flu epidemic." I figured that would soften his heart a little.

Instead he squinted at me. "Liz Bettencamp over at the village office says you was looking into that there stuff. I'd drop that if I was you, Nick. It's just being troublesome. Nobody wants that raised up. Won't bring nobody back from the dead."

"I've got a right to know about my ma and pa, haven't I?"

"Jack can tell you anything you need to know."

"Still, I want to take a look-see at the newspaper.

I can hitchhike home."

He tightened his lips. He wasn't going to let me wander around Millbury on my own, and I knew it. "How long you expect to be?"

"Not long," I said. I didn't know, really. "Fifteen minutes. Half hour, maybe."

"I'll wait, then." He wasn't taking any chances on me. He drove around to the library, and stood by a window where he could keep an eye on me.

I asked the librarian for copies of the *Millbury Gazette* for October 24 through 30, 1918. She brought them to me, and I sat at a table turning the pages. Each day the paper had a death list, mostly flu victims, just the name, address, age, and some relative—wife, daughter, whatever. I kept turning, watching for names, and then I found it. The story was headed UNKNOWN BOY FLU VICTIM. It said:

Stoneybeach village officials are looking for information concerning a boy named Jared Solters, age thirteen. He has been identified by a handwritten note found in his pocket giving his name and date of birth. The body was found October 24 on Bay Street, Stoneybeach. Stoneybeach First

Selectman Don Roberts said yesterday, "We're hoping to find a relative of the unfortunate boy."

That was all. It was enough, for Bay Street was our street. Not a very long street, either. Maybe twenty houses, where I lived with Uncle Jack, where he and Pa had grown up when my grandpa and grandma were alive.

I gave the newspapers back to the librarian, told Constable Tumulty that I was ready to go, and walked out of the library feeling cold and quiet.

A couple of days later in the middle of the afternoon Uncle Jack said he had an invite for coffee and cake over at Miss Bell's. I got a feeling he was going to talk to her about me—persuade her that there was another boy around who resembled me, so she wouldn't gossip about me around the village. He said I could have the rest of the afternoon off, so I went on out to Gypsy's. Mrs. Dauber was sitting in her rocker on the front porch, supposedly shelling peas, but mostly fanning herself with the *Millbury Gazette*. "Gypsy around?"

"Better be in the kitchen mopping the floor if she knows what's good for her tail," she said. I went around to the kitchen. For some reason I felt like being troublesome. "Having a good time, Gypsy?" I said.

She said a curse word a girl oughtn't to say. "Don't track your dirty feet on my wet floor." She swished the mop here and there in no particular order.

"That's an improvement," I said. "Move the dirt closer to the table rather than by the stove."

She gave me a look. "You better shut your mouth, Nick, or I'll push the mop in it."

"No, no," I said. "I meant it as a compliment. The dirt looks real nice over by the table. You can see it better. More light there than by the stove."

She took a swing at me with the mop. I jumped back and the mop caught a box of cornmeal that was sitting on the table. Cornmeal sprayed around the floor. She said the same curse word, only louder. "Now look what you made me do."

I laughed. "I didn't make you do it. You did it yourself."

"You're just being troublesome, Nick. Just for that, you can help me clean it up."

So we cleaned up the cornmeal. Then she flung the mop out into the backyard. "Let's get something to eat," she said.

"Okay," I said.

"There's some boiled potatoes and a chunk of salt beef in the icebox."

Cold boiled potatoes weren't my favorite, but I decided not to complain. She wrapped the stuff up in a piece of newspaper and stuck a bottle of sarsaparilla down her shirt. We were about to take off when Mrs. Dauber came into the kitchen, carrying the bowl of shelled peas. "What you got in that newspaper, Gypsy?"

"Another dead frog. The first one didn't work. Old Man Sneakers said we done it wrong—you got to warm it up in the sun before you throw it in the water. Then it'll come alive."

"Old Man Sneakers ought to warm hisself up in the sun before he opens his yap," Mrs. Dauber said. "I don't guess you two wouldn't feel more useful out there in the garden trying to warm up them weeds with a couple of hoes."

"We'd like to do it, Mrs. Dauber," I said, "but this is in the interest of science." That was a new expression I'd gotten out of the *Millbury Gazette*—some senator had said it when he got caught taking bribes from a medicine company. I figured if it was a good enough excuse for a senator, it was good enough for Mrs. Dauber.

"I'll science your hind end one of these days, Nick Hodges," she said. So off we went up the dusty road to our special clearing in the pine forest. We sat on the log and ate the boiled potatoes and boiled beef, which took some chewing. The sarsaparilla was a little more cheerful. Between mouthfuls I told Gypsy about the fingerprinting and all. Uncle Jack would have said I oughtn't to talk with my mouth full, but Gypsy didn't care and neither did I. Besides, Gypsy was keen to hear about the fingerprinting and wouldn't have wanted to wait until I swallowed. "The big thing is whether the other me has my fingerprints or not."

"Do you think he might?"

"No way to guess. But I can't wait around to find out. No two ways about it. If the fingerprints on that bucket match up with mine, they'll come after me right away. They're already scared I'll do something real bad. Once they see those prints, they'll have an excuse to lock me up somewhere."

The idea that I might go to jail was pretty interesting to her. Her pa got locked up from time to time for getting drunk and making a disturbance, but that was only overnight. Me getting locked up would be a bigger thing. "Where would they lock you up, Nick?"

"I don't know," I said. "I don't want to think about that. I've got to catch him first."

"You figured out a way yet?"

"Maybe," I said. "See, here's the thing. He can't go walking around the village unless he's sure I'm out of sight somewhere. He can't let anybody see me and him together. I figure he has to spend a lot of time up in the pine hills, just keeping out of the way. He can't take a chance on sleeping in the village, sneaking into a barn or shed and sleeping there. Since I found his shack, he's sure to have built himself another one in the pines somewhere. Of course I don't know if he has to sleep. Or eat, either. Maybe he doesn't. But if he's made of real flesh and bones, he probably does—need to eat and sleep."

"You sure he's flesh and bones, Nick? Maybe he's made out of some kind of magic stuff."

"Well, he felt real is all I can say. Got to stay out of the rain, anyway. But mainly he can't get caught in the same place I am. I figure he's either up there in the pines, or he's somewhere keeping an eye on me. Now here's what I figure. We—"

"What we? I don't wanna have nothin' to do

with your other. He scares the daylights out of me. Not like being scared of Pa when he comes home drunk—that's a regular kind of scared. This here other, he ain't regular. I tell you what he is, Nick. He's walking around dead. I don't wanna having nothin' to do with some walking dead guy. I wouldn't touch him for any amount of dough there is."

"Calm down, Gypsy. You don't have to touch him. I'll do that. Here's what we're going to do."

"I never agreed."

"Yes, you did," I said.

"When?"

"Just now," I said. "We're going to go up there, only we won't go together. We'll go separate by a hundred yards or some such, so he can't follow us both."

"I don't know how big a hundred yards is."

Neither did I. "I'll show you when we get there. If we can find his shack, we've got a chance to catch him sleeping. I'll bring some rope. See if we can catch him."

"What if he isn't up there sleeping?"

"If he isn't there, he'll be watching me. Bound to follow me, not you. You'll be going along separate from me, and you'll see him. Give me your owl call.

Then we'll wrestle him down and tie him up."

"I ain't gonna wrestle no dead guy, Nick."

"You have to. You said you would."

"I never did."

"We'll do it on Sunday after church."

"Maybe it'll rain."

"Stop worrying," I said.

But I knew it wasn't going to be as easy as I'd made out to Gypsy. If the other me was exactly as strong as me, Gypsy and me together could pin him down. But I didn't put any trust in that kind of logic—not when it came to something like this. Nothing sensible about it at all. That was part of what made it so scary: the rules were broken and the world was flying apart.

No matter how casual I was with Gypsy about it, like it didn't amount to anything at all, I wasn't looking forward to going after that other me— wrestling him down, tying him up, and such. I had a terrible feeling he was going to be too much for us. But I didn't see where I had a choice: I had to do it.

I was down in the boatyard the next morning helping Uncle Jack prise planks out of the hull of a boat that had gotten stove in, trying to put the other me out of my mind for the time being, when Constable Tumulty drove into the yard in his old Chevy with POLICE VILLAGE OF STONEYBEACH lettered on the side. He got out of the car, frowning somber. We stopped working and looked at him. "Well?" Uncle Jack said. "Came out the way I said, didn't it."

Constable Tumulty nodded. "You were right about that, Jack. I have to admit it. There was plenty of fingerprints on that bucket, but they wasn't Nick's."

I went light, and a smile came on me without my permission. I pulled it back, for I knew I had to take it seriously.

"Nick was here the whole time," Uncle Jack said. "I told you that."

The constable shook his head and went on frowning. "We still got our witness. Widow Clarke, she'll swear it was Nick. He wasn't but ten feet from her, stood there watching the fire flare up for four, five seconds."

"How do you account for the fingerprints, then, Ace?"

He shook his head once more. "I can't say. Maybe he was wearing gloves and Widow Clarke didn't notice—wouldn't be surprising, considering everything that was going on. Or maybe he put tape across his fingers. I'll tell you the truth—for your sake, Jack, I wished it wasn't Nick. But I can't disbelieve Widow Clarke. Living right across from the school the way she does, she knows all them kids. Chased 'em out of her yard often enough."

I was trying to stay out of it and let Uncle Jack do the arguing. But there was something I understood about it that they didn't. "Constable, why would I stand around like that so Widow Clarke could get a good look at me? Make more sense if I ran off in the other direction, out back toward the old orchard there. Why run right by the widow's house where she could see me?"

Uncle Jack gave me a long look while something worked in his mind. "Ace, Nick thinks there's a kid showed up in Stoneybeach the last couple of weeks or so who looks like him. Close resemblance, anyway."

The constable squinted one eye at Jack and then at me. "Jack, that's about the worst excuse I ever heard."

It'd been a mistake to bring that up, for if we were making up excuses for it, I must be guilty. I decided to keep my mouth shut.

"Either way," Uncle Jack said, "Nick's finger-prints weren't on that bucket. Nor did Widow Clarke say anything about him wearing gloves or anything. How're you going to explain that in court?"

Constable Tumulty stood there pulling on his chin, saying nothing for a minute. Then he said, "Well, there *was* something funny about them fin-gerprints. Wasn't Nick's, that's the fact. But the fella that does the fingerprinting over there at the state cops in Millbury, he said it was the dangedest thing he ever saw. Them prints looked like Nick's—only backward. Reversed. He said he didn't notice it at first. It was only when he studied them awhile that he began to wonder. So he held them up to a mirror, and there it was. In a mirror, them prints are identi-cal to Nick's. The fella said he was so surprised, his teeth almost fell out. Identical, down to the tiniest loop and whorl. Said he'd never seen anything like it."

I went cold inside. Uncle Jack looked at me, kind of puzzled. Then he looked back at the constable. "Ace, did this fingerprint fella say there was any way you could do that—turn your fingerprints around like that?"

"Oh, you can bet I asked him. We went over that thorough. Finally he said he'd call down to Washington. He called me back this morning. Down there they told him they'd never heard anything like it. Said there was ways you could probably do it in a fingerprint lab if you had the right equipment, but not some kid running along with a galvanized bucket."

"So it's just a coincidence."

The constable went on pulling his chin. Finally he said, "Mighty big coincidence is all I can say. If it'd been just one finger, or a couple of 'em, I'd say coincidence. But four fingers and a thumb on both hands?" He gave me a look. "You got lucky this time, Nick. I don't know how you done it. But there better not be any next time." And he got in the Chevy and drove away.

Uncle Jack stood there looking at me for a little while. Then he said, "Well, this isn't getting that stove-in boat fixed," and we set to work again.

I had trouble working that day. I kept thinking this can't be happening to me. It was like I was trying to run through a dark woods with the rain dropping, the wind roaring, the branches of the trees slashing at me, catching at me so'd I pull away from

116

one that was hooked into my shirt and another one would grab at my arm. I had to get rid of him. I had to catch him somehow, and get rid of him.

So no matter how scared I felt, I was mighty glad when Sunday finally came around, for I'd be doing something about it at last. After lunch Uncle Jack went down to the boatyard to finish up a few things. I said I might go out to Gypsy's. I waited until he was gone. Then I went out to the toolshed behind the house and found a nice piece of half-inch rope about ten feet long. I wrapped it around myself under my shirt, and then I headed on out to Gypsy's.

She didn't want to go—it was too much to ask. She kept looking up at the sky. "It might rain, Nick," she said.

"There isn't a cloud up there, Gypsy. Nothing but blue."

"Sometimes a storm comes up just like that. Blue sky one minute and pouring rain the next."

I didn't much feel like arguing over the weather. "If you don't come, I'm going to do it alone and you can forget about being my friend."

So she came, scuffling her feet along and looking down at the ground. "Cut it out, Gypsy. I'm the one they're going to trample on, not you."

We came to the cemetery and she got more interested. "Where's this here boy buried?" she said.

"Over there." We went over. "See?" I said. "See how the earth's all scuffed up?"

Gypsy looked around, and then touched a piece of scuffed-up sod with her toe, real easy, like she was testing a dead snake. "You figure he come up out of there, Nick?"

"I don't figure anything. I don't know what the truth of it is."

She kicked the turf a little harder and looked serious. "Mighty hard for a kid our age to die like that. All alone with nobody to help him die. Nobody to cover him up with a blanket when he was shivering and tell him the worst was over and he'd soon be on his feet, so he'd feel better about being dead." She shivered and put her arms around herself.

I felt like shivering myself, but I didn't. "Come on, let's go." We climbed over the stone wall and walked out through the hardwood stand until we got to where the pine forest began and the ground began to rise up. "Hold still," I said. I took a long look around in all directions, listening carefully. Nothing. Was he up in the pine hills? Or was he somewhere behind us, lying in the shadows, watching us? "You wait here, Gypsy. Count to five hundred, slow. Then come on after me. If you see him, give your owl call. Then we'll close in on him."

She shivered again. "I don't wanna touch him, Nick."

"I already touched him, Gypsy. He feels the same as you and me. Now, let's cut out the talk. I'm going. Start counting."

I set off through the pine forest, moving as quick as I could without making too much noise. I was pretty well nerved up and kept taking deep breaths to calm myself down. The ground was getting steeper. Here and there the forest broke where a rough gray rock ledge came up out of the ground. After a bit I came to his old shack. Window was gone from it; so was the blanket from the door. He'd built himself another shack somewhere. I glanced in. Nothing. I went on.

Every few minutes I stopped to look and listen—see if I could hear him moving through the pines. Take only half a minute over it, so Gypsy wouldn't catch up with me, and then move on again.

I went on like that for a good twenty minutes. There was more ledge up there, so that the forest was thinner and a good deal of light came through.

I was going along like this when I heard the owl call.

I jumped and stopped dead. My sweat went cold. The owl call came again. Gypsy wasn't making any secret of it. It meant that not only had she spotted the other me, but that the other had spotted her. I turned and ran back down toward where the owl call came from. I hadn't gone more than fifty feet when I saw him.

He was standing on a ledge about twenty feet long and maybe six feet high. He'd picked a good spot because if we rushed him, even from two directions, he'd be able to leap off the ledge in a third direction and disappear into the pines.

I was an easy stone's throw from him. He was grinning and dancing around on the ledge, mighty happy with himself. The sun was splashing down on him so I could see him clear—had on a shirt like mine, only buttoned wrong-way to. I stood still, so as not to spook him, trying to think of a way we would catch him.

He went on dancing. "Thought you'd catch me, didn't you, Nick? Not this time, old buddy. Thought you were slick, but you're not slick enough for me, Nick Hodges." He did a couple more dance steps.

It gave me the strangest feeling to watch myself

dancing around crazy like that, and hearing my own voice come out of somebody else's mouth.

Gypsy came up beside me. "Holy moly, Nick," she said. "He's you."

"Oh yes I am," the other me said. He went on dancing on the ledge in the sunlight. "I sure am." He laughed and looked at Gypsy. "That owl call didn't fool me for one minute. I knew in two seconds it wasn't any owl. Here they come, these fools, hoping to box me up like those chickens, but they don't know me." He jumped up and kicked out his legs. "Don't know me at all."

I wanted to get him talking, so he'd let down his guard. "Listen," I said. "Why're you after me especially? I never did you any harm." It was like talking to myself.

He stopped dancing and spit off the ledge. "Oh yes you did, Nick Hodges. Oh yes you did, and I'm going to get you for it. You know I am." He grinned and started dancing again.

"I'm scared, Nick," Gypsy said. "Let's go."

I was plenty scared myself, but I wasn't going to go. "Are you Jared Solters?"

He went on dancing. "How could I be Jared Solters. He died, didn't he? He's dead, isn't he? How could I be him?"

I couldn't answer that. "Okay," I said. "Whatever I did to you, I didn't mean it. I'm sorry. What can I do to make it right?"

He stopped dancing. "Make it right? Oh, don't worry about that, I'll make it right. Don't you worry about that." He started dancing again.

"You want to get me killed, don't you."

"Oh, and I'm going to, Nick Hodges. No two ways about it. Don't you worry yourself on that score."

He was even using some of my expressions. "Why do you want to be me? I'm nobody special. Don't have a ma and pa, just my uncle. Got to work like anyone else. It isn't so great to be me."

"You think I got a ma and pa?" He frowned and looked sullen. "Weren't any use to me when I had them, either. Pretty quick with his fists, Pa was."

"Still, being me isn't too great," I said.

"Want to change places, old buddy?"

I couldn't answer that. "What use is it to you to get me killed?"

"Don't you worry about that, Nick."

"Aren't you afraid I might kill you first?"

He went on dancing. "You'll have a hard time

doing that, old buddy."

It wasn't working. Nothing was working. I took a deep breath. "How'd you manage to steal my reflection?"

"Oh, I have my ways."

"Why mine? Why not somebody else's?"

He stopped dancing. The grin went from his face and a dark scowl came on his face. "Why don't you ask your uncle Jack about that?" he said. Then he shook his fist, jumped off the ledge into the pine forest, and was gone. It was his left fist that he'd shaken.

Chapter Seven

Lying in my bed that night with my arms behind my head, I thought about it. Somehow I had to lure him out into the village where there were some people around. Didn't have to be a lot of people; a few would be enough. Three or four fishermen down on the wharf. People drinking coffee in Miss Bell's pastry shop. Someplace where I could be hiding and jump out when the other me turned up, so the people would see us together. But how was I going to do that?

The other question was, what did Uncle Jack have to do with it? From what the other me said, Uncle Jack was part of it. In fact, now that I got to thinking about it, the other me was blaming Uncle

Jack for it more than he was me.

But there was no way to believe that Uncle Jack had harmed anybody. He always said he'd seen enough hurting during the war to last a lifetime—people stabbing each other with bayonets, filling some poor fella hung up on barbwire with machine-gun bullets. Stuff like that. Uncle Jack would do anything for anybody. Miss Bell was always saying he was too much of a saint, he ought to look out for himself more. That wasn't Uncle Jack's way.

I spent the next couple of days thinking it over. I still hadn't come up with anything when Miss Bell came over to play cribbage a couple of nights later. They set up on the little table in the parlor. I knew Miss Bell didn't want me hanging around, so I plunked myself down on the parlor sofa with the *Millbury Gazette*, innocent as a cat. I made sure to make a good deal of noise when I turned the pages. To add to Miss Bell's enjoyment, from time to time I'd read out a little story that was in the paper, especially if it was boring. You know, "It says here in the paper that they're going to put a stop sign on Slater Street where that car accident was," or "It says here in the paper that the Millbury Village selectmen have decided to put off painting town hall because of the expense."

Finally it got to where she couldn't stand it anymore. She gave me as good a smile as she could work up, considering her feelings. "Nick, I'm sure this is boring for you. I'll pay you fifty cents to go down to my pastry shop and give the bakery floor a good scrubbing. And there's some leftover apricot tarts in the cupboard that aren't going to any good use."

"Oh, I wasn't bored, Miss Bell," I said. But fifty cents and a free hand with a plateful of tarts for scrubbing a floor was too good to turn down. "Still, I don't mind being helpful." She squeezed out another smile, gave me the keys to the shop, and off I went.

I'd done cleaning for Miss Bell before, and I knew where everything was. It didn't take me more than twenty minutes to do the floor, and because part of the deal was for me to stay away for awhile, I polished up the glass in her display cases, tidied up a bit, and then got down the apricot tarts and went to work on them. So it was a good hour, maybe a little more, before I shut off the lights and went out. I locked the door and started for home when I noticed somebody up ahead a ways walking quickly along—somebody about my size.

He was moving fast, crouching down a little, and keeping out of the lights shining from the houses along the way.

He'd made a mistake: hadn't figured I'd leave the pastry shop so soon. Suddenly I saw that I had a chance to get him. My heart began to race and my breath to come quick. Instead of following him along, I turned off at the next corner and began to run until I came to Oak Street. I turned up Oak, still running, crossed Bay Street, and circled around the block until I could come up to our house through the backyard. I slipped in among the lilac bushes there, crouched in the shadows, and looked toward the kitchen.

Through the windows I could see Uncle Jack and Miss Bell in the kitchen. Uncle Jack was heating up coffee. Miss Bell got down a couple of coffee mugs from the cupboard, set them on the wooden kitchen table, went over to the stove, put her hand on Uncle Jack's arm, and said something I couldn't hear.

Then I heard the front door bang open. I came up out of my crouch, running. As I crossed the lawn I saw the other me come ambling into the kitchen. I had my hand on the kitchen doorknob and was just about to open it when Miss Bell turned her back to me to face the other me. "Finished already, Nick?" she said.

The other me began to dance. "I'll tell what's finished," he said. "I'm finished with you coming around here like you owned the place, trying to get Jack to marry you."

Miss Bell gasped, and Uncle Jack's mouth dropped open. "Nick, I don't believe what I heard," he said.

Miss Bell cried, "Believe it, Jack. I told you all along the boy's gone to the bad."

I swung open the kitchen door. Already Miss Bell had turned away and was pushing past the other me out of the kitchen toward the front door. Then she was gone. The other me went on dancing. "Out you go, fatso," he shouted.

I saw now I ought to have gotten there a half minute sooner. I stopped in the middle of the kitchen. Uncle Jack flung himself against the kitchen wall like he'd been hit, his mouth open wide. He looked at the other me, back at me, and then at the other me again. But the other me was dashing past us and out through the kitchen door. I charged after him, but he had too much of a head start for me, and in a flash he was across the backyard and racing away.

I went back into the kitchen. Uncle Jack was still standing against the kitchen wall, looking shocked. "Well," he said. "Well."

He poured himself a mug of coffee, and I noticed his hand was shaking. He sat down at the kitchen table and I sat opposite him. For a minute he stared down into his coffee. Then he raised his head up. "Do you know who he is?"

"I'm not sure," I said. It was a relief to have it out in the open. "I think he might have had something to do with a kid who died in the flu epidemic."

He turned his head to look out the window into the darkness. Then he turned back. "A lot of kids died. I missed most of it, because I was in that hospital in England when it hit Stoneybeach."

"A boy named Jared Solters."

He turned to look out into the darkness again. "Yes, I remember him. Nobody knew where he came from. We took a collection to put up a gravestone for him." He went on looking out the window. There was something he wanted to say, but he wasn't sure if he should. Finally he looked back at me. "That's all you know about him, Nick? Nothing more than that?"

"A little," I said. "When I was working on the

cemetery awhile back, I noticed Jared's gravestone was knocked over and the dirt over the grave scuffed up. I set it up, for I knew I'd get blamed. I saw this other me at the edge of the woods. The next chance I got I traced him up into the pines and found this little shack he'd built. He moved farther back after that—I don't know where. So Gypsy and me went out looking for him. He must have been watching us the whole time, because suddenly he came out on a ledge where we couldn't get at him and started dancing around and taunting us." I paused, looked away, and then looked back at Uncle Jack. "He said you would know why he was making trouble for me."

He didn't answer me, but looked out the window again. Finally he said, "I better go see Emma Bell. I don't want her spreading this all over town. She's as good as a newspaper for putting things around."

"It won't do any good, Uncle Jack. She didn't see me come in. She was already running out. She'll say you're covering up for me, same as Constable Tumulty thinks."

"Maybe," he said. "I'm going to try, anyway."

I was too nervous to sit, too nervous to do anything, really, but walk around, back and forth from the kitchen to the parlor, around the kitchen table, and back into the parlor. In a way, things were better, for Uncle Jack knew the truth of it now. But mainly it was much worse. Miss Bell was going to spread the story all over town—chances as good as this to make yourself the center of attention didn't grow on trees. It'd get worse each time she told it. In the first version I'd be cursing and swearing; in the third version I'd have grown horns and a tail; in the sixth version I'd have grown seven feet tall and shot electric bolts at her from my eyes. Once she got finished, I'd be blamed for anything that went wrong in Stoneybeach—fire, robbery, murder, they'd say Nick Hodges must have done it. Wouldn't matter if it had been impossible for me to do it—fishing boat capsized in a storm twenty miles at sea while I was over at Millbury getting a tooth drilled in front of six witnesses, they'd say I'd managed it some way.

I was in pretty big trouble. The people of Stoneybeach were already fed up with me. Once Miss Bell started telling them I'd gone crazy, they'd want to get rid of me as soon as they could. Where would I go? What would I do?

Finally Uncle Jack came back. He sat down at the

kitchen table. "You were right, Nick. She figures I'm covering up for you. She said the same as Ace Tumulty; she understands how I feel, but I have to face the fact that you've gone off your head and are a danger to people. I tried to explain about this other one. Didn't push it too hard, just said there's a boy around who looks a lot like you, but of course that's pretty hard to believe. Wouldn't have believed it if I hadn't seen it myself. I told her that I know the story isn't sensible, but that it is true nonetheless. She said people in town have to be warned. I begged her to hold off saying anything for a bit until I could think about the whole thing. She won't. She said people have got to be warned. She'll blab it all over the village."

"Uncle Jack, you know what I think? I think he worked this out so he could draw you into it. Whatever happened to him that's making him so evil, he blames you for it, too. I think he's trying to draw you into it, so people around here'll go after you, too."

He thought about it. "Maybe," he said. "Pretty smart of him if it's true."

"Well, like when he set that fire up at the school. He must have known I was working at the boatyard with you at that moment. Like he knew I was at the pastry shop tonight, mopping out the bakery floor. He has his eye on me a good deal. And if he knew I was there in the boatyard with you when he set that fire, he must have realized you'd catch on to him. He could have waited to set the fire until sometime when I was off somewhere."

Uncle Jack considered. "Maybe," he said. "Maybe he wants to draw me in. But it doesn't do to jump to conclusions. There's too much mystery in this."

"What do you think they're likely to do to me?"

"You mean people around here?" He thought about it, rubbing his chin. "I don't know. Legally, not much as of now. Insulting Emma Bell isn't a criminal offense, and their case on the school fire isn't too good, not with somebody else's finger-prints on that bucket. But I don't doubt that the other boy will try to pin something worse on you. The worrisome part is if some of the fellas decide to take the law into their own hands. One thing I learned out of the war, you can take a bunch of fine fellas, type of men who always helped old ladies across the street and were the first one to cough up a dollar when a neighbor was in trouble; get a bunch of such fine fellas to where they think they got a grievance, some injustice done to them as they see it, and they'll turn into animals. Turn into a pack of wolves and tear apart the first poor creature they come across."

"What injustice is there around Stoneybeach, Uncle Jack? What grievance have they got?"

Uncle Jack shrugged. "Nick, most everybody thinks they have a grievance. Most everybody thinks they ought to have done better for themselves—made more money, gotten a bigger house, or a better husband or wife, be better thought of around town. You ever meet anybody who thought he was the luckiest fella on earth?"

I thought about it. "No, I don't reckon I have."

"You won't, either. Everybody figures they would have done better one way or another if something hadn't gone wrong. Once I figured that one out, I took life a little more easy. Try to take things as they come. Sometimes things are going to be hard, and there's no use complaining. There's always people who've got it worse."

"Uncle Jack, I'm scared they're going to run me out of town."

He gave me a little smile to comfort me. "Let's not worry about that yet, Nick. We've got to put on our thinking caps."

Two mornings later when we were putting a primer coat of paint on the new planks we'd put in the stove-in boat, Constable Tumulty drove into the yard in his police Chevy. I knew right away it was trouble and so did Uncle Jack, for he put down his brush. "I'd like to talk to you alone, Jack," the constable said.

"I don't guess there's anything we can't discuss right here, Ace."

The constable shook his head. "I'd rather talk alone."

Uncle Jack shrugged and they went into the shop. I was mighty curious, but I figured Uncle Jack would tell me about it. Fifteen minutes later they came out. Uncle Jack said, "Nick, Constable Tumulty wants you to talk to a doc over in Millbury. They want to see if you're crazy."

"Now Jack," Constable Tumulty said, "that ain't a helpful way of puttin' it."

"I don't aim to be helpful," Uncle Jack said. "I know Nick. I know he isn't crazy. You're going off half cocked about this."

"He threatened to kill Emma Bell, Jack."

"That's Emma's story. It isn't what I heard and I

was there, too."

I knew I ought to keep my mouth shut, but I was getting mad. "She say I grew horns and a tail?" I said.

The constable snapped his head around and stared at me. Clear enough she'd said something like that—I was full of the devil, or had got taken over by Satan. "Let's not argue over it, Jack. Let the doc decide."

"What if I refuse?" Uncle Jack said.

Constable Tumulty shrugged. "I'll take it to Justice Maloney. Nick's got a pretty bad reputation around here now. People are after me to do something about it. Can't say as I blame them. Maloney'll give me a court order."

Uncle Jack was more angry than I'd seen him for a long while, but he kept hold of himself. "Ace, I could go to Maloney myself and argue my side of it, but I don't guess I'd do any good. You'll find out for yourself soon enough." He turned and strode away.

The constable looked at me. I could tell he was worried I might try to fight him off. But I knew there wasn't any point in that—I'd just get myself put in handcuffs, maybe get banged around a little in the bargain. So I got into the car and we started for Millbury.

Uncle Jack figured the doc would see that I wasn't crazy, but I wasn't so sure. It seemed like people didn't need much evidence to decide something was wrong with you. What, really, was the evidence against me? They couldn't blame the school fire on me, because the fingerprints on that galvanized bucket weren't mine. So what did they have? Broke some windows in the church, mouthed off at Miss Bell a couple of times. It wasn't serious enough. Troublesome, sure; but they'd always believed I was troublesome. That wasn't anything new. Of course most of them still believed I'd set the school on fire. Didn't matter that I *couldn't* have— couldn't have carried that bucket around like that without getting my fingerprints all over it. But they believed it anyway.

It was almost like they *wanted* to believe I was crazy. Had a wish to believe that somebody around was taken over by the devil. Well, I don't know how many of them believed in the devil—some of them, most likely. So I had to be got rid of. Locked up somewhere. Killed, even.

I thought about that. Would they really, actually kill me? Not yet, anyway. Not until I'd done something worse. And that was coming, for I was sure that the other me wouldn't rest until he'd gotten rid of me, and Uncle Jack, too, if he could.

We got over to Millbury soon enough. The doc's office was up over a drugstore in the middle of town. On his door it said in gold letters, DR. WERNER ESSEN, PEDIATRIC MEDICINE. We went into the waiting room. There was nobody there. We sat and waited, and in about fifteen minutes the doc opened a door and smiled at us. He nodded to me in a friendly way and held the door open for me to go into his office. There wasn't much to see: a desk, table, pictures of flowers on the walls, a rug on the floor. He told me to sit down at the table, and he sat down opposite me.

The whole thing was making me pretty nervous. Things were happening to me that I had no say in, and couldn't do anything about.

First thing the doc did was show me some cards that had black blotches on them. I was supposed to say what they looked like. "They look like black blotches," I told him. However, that wasn't what I was supposed to say. I was supposed to see something in the blotches, like a cloud, an upside-down cow, and so forth. He made notes on a pad about what I said. When we got done with that, he showed me some pictures of various people—a couple of kids talking, a man and a woman in a room, and so forth. For these I was supposed to figure out what they were saying to each other. With the kind of mind I had, I was bound to think of weird things for them to say—like the man was telling the woman that her nose was moving around on her face, or the two kids were deciding to sew their shirts together and pretend they were Siamese twins. But I knew better than to say stuff like that, so I said that the man and the woman were talking about which movie to go to, and them kids were planning to build a tree house. The doc took notes on this, too.

After the pictures, he asked me some questions in a way that was supposed to be friendly. "Now, Nick, this boy you believe to be imitating you. You've seen him."

I told myself to be careful. Better not make too much of it. "Yes. My uncle Jack saw him, too."

"How close were you to him?"

I figured he didn't know about me seeing the other me in the woods, just that time in our kitchen. "About from here to your desk," I said. "Pretty close. Like I said, Uncle Jack saw him, too."

He wasn't interested in what Uncle Jack saw. "Were you able to touch him?"

"No. He ran off before we could do anything."

"What were you going to do?"

I saw I'd said too much. "I don't know. Try to catch him, I guess. If you had somebody jumping in on you all the time, you'd want to catch him to find out was going on. Anybody would."

"Did he say anything?"

I was beginning to get the idea behind his questions. He already believed there wasn't any such thing as the other me, so anything I said about him must be crazy. "No. He didn't say anything to me."

"Did he say something to anyone else?"

He was trying to hem me in. "He ran off about ten seconds after I came in."

"But you got a good look at him."

"Not too good," I said.

"He looked like you, though."

Whatever I said in answer to that would be wrong. "Well, a good deal, yes."

"Close resemblance."

"Yes."

"Like a twin."

If I said yes, he'd take me for crazy, and if I said no, nothing else I'd said would make any sense. "I don't know about a twin. Pretty close resemblance." I was never going to convince him. I took a deep breath. "People take him for me, anyway."

"But nobody ever sees him when you're there."

"That's not true," I said. "Like I keep saying, my uncle Jack saw us when we were both in the kitchen."

He nodded. "Yes, so I understand." He watched me closely. "But nobody else. Miss Bell was there at the time and didn't see him. She didn't see a double, a twin, anything like that."

"She's a blame liar. She wasn't there. She was leaving, going out the front door when I was coming in the back door. She was mad as a hornet and ran out without turning around. She didn't see me come in." I realized I was losing control of myself. It was the unfairest thing I'd ever gotten into. I took a deep breath to catch hold of myself.

"According to her, you shouted something about her wanting to marry your Uncle Jack."

"I never said any such thing." I knew he wasn't going to believe it.

"Uncle Jack is very important to you, isn't he, Nick."

"Well, sure," I said. "What's wrong with that?"

"Nothing at all wrong with it, Nick." He paused. "If he should marry, it'd disturb your relationship with him, wouldn't it. You might lose him to her."

So that was it. "Why do I care if Uncle Jack marries Miss Bell? It might be nice to have her for a ma." It wouldn't be nice, but I wasn't going to say that.

He nodded, made a note on his pad, and that was the end of it. Constable Tumulty drove me home. A couple of times he asked me how it had gone, trying to get something out of me, but all I said was "Okay."

Uncle Jack got the report a couple of days later. "The doc phoned Ace Tumulty. He's sending a formal report to Justice Maloney. He says you're suffering from paranoid delusions."

"What's that?"

"I don't know exactly. I'm not up on that stuff. I guess it means you're seeing things. Seeing enemies all around when there aren't any there."

"But you saw him, Uncle Jack. So did Gypsy."

"Nobody around here believes a word any of the

Daubers say."

"Why not? What'd Gypsy do wrong?"

"It isn't so much that she did anything wrong," he said. "The way people see it, the Daubers don't fit in right. Folks around here like to see people live tidy. You couldn't say that of the Daubers."

That was true enough. "They don't believe you, either, Uncle Jack."

"They figure I'm covering up for you."

Neither of us said anything. Then I said, "What do they want to do to me?"

"They want to lock you up, Nick. They want to put you in a mental home and keep you there."

"But I didn't do anything," I shouted.

"They think you did."

"Even if it was me, the only thing I did was bust a few windows in the church and speak up to Miss Bell a couple of times. That's not so bad."

He put a hand on my shoulder to calm me down. "They're not listening to reason anymore, Nick," he said, looking mighty serious. "It's the way people are. They've made up their minds that something's gotten into you. I'm not supposed to know what they're saying, but it gets back to me. Some people think it's the devil, plain out. Most of them wouldn't put it quite so strong. Say you were a bad seed. Say you were always a little bit off. However they put it, they want to get rid of you."

"Can they do it? Lock me up somewhere?"

"They'll need a court order. That'll take a few days, maybe longer. I'm going to fight it, of course. Talk to a lawyer." He squeezed my shoulder. "We're not dead yet, Nick."

I wished he hadn't put it that way.

Chapter Eight

What would it be like to be in a mental home? Pretty bad, I figured. Not that I knew firsthand, but I'd seen stuff about mental homes in movies and books. People shrieked and moaned all night. If they got loose, they'd go after you with whatever they could lay their hands on—broken bottle, leg off a chair. I read this story once where some man in a mental home got cornered by a lunatic. So long as he stared the lunatic in the eye, the lunatic would hold off; but if he got sleepy and let his eyes droop, the lunatic would be on him. I shivered. And I might be stuck there forever.

Uncle Jack knew how I was feeling, and he gave me the afternoon off so I could go out to Gypsy's. I guess he figured the time might be coming when I wouldn't be seeing Gypsy at all. I walked on out. At least it was a nice sunny day. The birds were chirping and flashing among the trees. Some crows were cawing over a big discovery they'd made; blue jays were being bossy; here and there a cardinal or a goldfinch sliced red or gold through the branches. A little breeze was coming off the bay. Everything was real nice, and I decided to enjoy it if I could.

Gypsy was up in the truck garden picking pole beans. "Ma's going to put some up. Then we're going to do the tomatoes." She paused. "Pa's home."

"Is he okay?"

"He says he's reformed for good," she said.

"You believe it, Gypsy?"

"I'll believe it until he ain't reformed no more. What'd that doc you went to say?"

"He said I was crazy. I had delusions and ought to be locked up."

"Locked up?" She stopped picking beans and stared at me. "In jail?"

"Not in jail," I said. "In a mental home. It's scary. If I spend a lot of time with people who howl at the moon or think they're the King of France, I'll get pretty crazy myself."

"Nick, they can't do that."

"Uncle Jack says they might be able to. I don't know if I'll ever get out. I can't believe that something like that would happen to me. It doesn't seem real. It seems like it must be happening to somebody else, not me. I can't believe it."

"Well, that other guy is real. I saw him."

"If you and Uncle Jack hadn't seen him, I'd have been sure I was crazy. I'd have had to kill myself."

She looked frightened. "Nick, don't say that. Who'd I have to talk to? Everybody in town hates us. They look down on us because of Pa."

"Why are you so worried about who you'd talk to? Who'd I talk to?" I shook myself. "Well, I won't do it—won't kill myself. Not yet, anyway. Let's talk about something else. You think your pa'll really reform?"

"Naw," she said. "Not him."

I helped her pick beans and listened to her chatter away, and when we got a couple of buckets full of beans, we went down to the house in hopes there'd be something lying around worth swiping. Instead, Mr. Dauber was sitting in his undershirt at the kitchen table, drinking a glass of sarsaparilla.

"Nice to see young folks busy," he said, scratching his armpits. "Idle hands make the devil's work."

"In that case, Pa," Gypsy said, "whyn't you come on out to the garden and help us pick the pole beans, so the devil can't get at you?"

"I would," he said seriously, "but I've got some thinking to do. Nick, tell your uncle Jack that I'm a reformed man. Changed for good. Gone over to the Lord's side. Going back on the fishing boats the way I done when I was young. Big mistake to quit fishing. Figured I'd do better over to Millbury in the paper mills, but it wasn't so. Should have known better. Tell your uncle to put the word out to the fellas that there's a real good hand in want of a job." He shook his head to let me know he was serious. "Now, you remember to tell him, hear, Nick?"

He was so busy talking to me about his reform that he missed seeing Gypsy take a handful of cookies out of the cookie jar and drop them in the bean bucket. "Come on, Nick," she said.

"Now, you tell your uncle Jack I'm a reformed fella. Gone over to the Lord."

When I got home I told Uncle Jack about Mr. Dauber being reformed and looking for work on the fishing boats. All he said was "Humph." But

Rev. Clampett told Frank Sanders that out of Christian charity he ought to give Mr. Dauber a second chance. "I don't mind giving a man a second chance," Frank Sanders said, "but a twentieth chance is stretching it." However, he took Mr. Dauber on, and to everyone's surprise Mr. Dauber began turning up sober on the wharf every morning.

Meanwhile, Uncle Jack went over to Millbury to see a lawyer somebody had told him about. He got back at suppertime, and we sat there eating our beans and brown bread in the red light from the setting sun bouncing off the white kitchen walls.

"This here lawyer doubts that any judge'd lock you up in a mental home on the say-so of one doc. Most likely want you tested again. Get the opinion of two, three docs. The lawyer says they got to show where you're a danger to others, or a danger to yourself. If you were crazy but weren't harming anyone, there'd be no cause to lock you up. Like Old Man Sneakers—he doesn't make much sense half the time, but he's no trouble to anyone. They can't lock you up for not making sense. If they could, half the world'd be in a mental home."

"What if they get a couple more docs to say I'm crazy?"

"No point in borrowing trouble, Nick. It's Ace Tumulty's move. I don't doubt but what some folks in town are after him to lock you up, but he's got a ways to go before he does that. First step is to get you tested a couple more times. Then go to court. The lawyer will cross-examine the docs. He says sometimes you get a judge who doesn't hold with a lot of this psychology stuff. You never know." He squinted his eyes and shook his head, like he was hurting someplace. "I just wish I could make more sense out of it, Nick. There's got to be a reasonable explanation for it, but I'm blamed if I can think of one. I'll be honest, when I saw the two of you standing side by side, it took the wind out of my sails. Threw me for a loop. Didn't know where I was for a minute there."

"If it weren't for Miss Bell, I wouldn't be in all this trouble."

"Don't be too hard on Emma. You heard what this double of yours said to her."

"She doesn't have to lie about it."

"No, she shouldn't do that." He nodded his head slowly, and then he looked at me. "Nick, I think there's something about all of this you haven't told me."

I looked him straight back. He was smart, all right. "All right. I'll tell you. I was afraid it'd make me sound crazy." I didn't have anything to lose anymore. I took a deep breath. "I don't have any reflection any more. He took it."

Uncle Jack leaned forward, his eyes wide, staring into my face. "You don't have any reflection?"

"No," I said. "Not in a mirror, not in a shop window, not in a pool of still water." I stood up. "I'll show you." I went into the bathroom, and he came along behind me. It was a tight fit for the two of us in there. I stood in front of the old sink with its yellow stains, facing the mirror. He stood behind me, looking over my head. The mirror showed only his face.

"Good God," he said. He never swore in front of me, but this slipped out. "I don't believe it." He moved a little from one side to the next, hoping I'd come into view from a different angle. But I didn't. He went back out of the bathroom, lit the stove under the coffeepot, and stood frowning over it until it had heated up. He poured himself a cup of coffee and came back to the table. For a long time he said nothing, just stared down at his coffee cup. Finally he said, "When did you first notice this?"

"That first day, when Miss Bell said I'd walked by her without speaking at Briggs Pond. Gypsy and me went over there to have a look around and I noticed it then."

"And it's been that way right along?"

"Yes." I waited for him to say something. But he didn't, just looked out the window. So I said, "I figured this Jared Solters got it somehow. It's what he's made of."

He sat there frowning down into his coffee again for the longest time, just frowning and thinking while his coffee grew cold. I didn't move, didn't say anything, but sat there, too. We sat while the red light faded off the walls and the kitchen began to get dark. Finally he stood up and turned on the light that hung over the kitchen table. He picked up his coffee cup and began to walk around the room. "This here Jared Solters." He stopped pacing and looked at me. "You don't have any idea who he is?"

"Some. When I was over at Millbury being fingerprinted, I got the constable to take me to the library. I combed through the old newspapers and found a story where it said he'd died in the epidemic over on our street. It said they were looking for his folks."

He nodded. "That's about the size of it, I guess."

"It had something to do with us, didn't it, Uncle Jack?"

He came back over to the table and sat down, one hand hanging on to the coffee cup. He stared out the window into the backyard. Twilight was coming, but light was still shining on the lilac bushes at the back of the yard.

"The way it was, Nick, over there in France, in September, there was this big push—Americans, British, French—into the Argonne forest. That's when I got hit. Busted up my arm and shoulder pretty good. They sent me back to a hospital in England. I stayed there until I was healed up enough to travel, and they sent me back to the United States for convalescent leave. I'd have had to've gone back to France but the war ended.

"All the time I was in the hospital I hadn't got any mail—it just didn't catch up to me. Over there we knew that the flu had hit pretty bad, but we didn't know how bad. I guess they didn't want us doughboys worrying that our folks back home might be dying. So I didn't know how bad it had been in Stoneybeach. Landed in New York, took the train up to Boston, and then another one to Millbury, and hitched a ride over to Stoneybeach. The fella who gave me a ride kind of hinted that things had been bad around here, but I was so glad to get home I didn't pay much attention. Looking forward to seeing your pa and ma, my old friends and such. Fella dropped me off at the wharf. Frankie Sanders and a couple of others were there. They came over and stood around hemming and hawing, and finally Frankie had to spill it out: the flu had hit Stoneybeach pretty hard, and your pa and ma were dead and had been buried a couple of weeks before.

"I got the house, the boatyard, and you. I was still awkward with my arm and wasn't able to work yet, but I had some back pay and could manage." He looked at me and gave a little smile. "Had a heck of a time changing your diapers with one arm, I recall."

He looked back out the window. The light was about gone, mostly shadows out there. "But the flu was still everywhere. Somebody sick in half the houses in Stoneybeach. Most of them got better, of course, but a lot died. It seemed like the church bell never stopped ringing. People stayed home as much as they could, but they had their jobs to go to. Seeing as I wasn't able to work yet, I didn't go out any more than I had to. Didn't want to risk bringing back flu germs to you. I knew that'd be the worst thing I could do to your ma and pa. All they had left out of their lives was you—you were what their lives amounted to. I wasn't going to risk you. Only went out to stock up on food, kerosene. Stayed put otherwise."

He'd never talked about any of this before. Never talked about being wounded or coming home to find everybody dead. For the first time I could see why he'd been willing to take me on—he did it for his brother. Did it for me, too, I figured, but at the beginning he didn't know me enough to have any feeling for me. That must have come over time. "You could have sent me to an orphan home," I said.

"Yes, I could have. A lot of people said I should. Said it wasn't right for a young fella who had served his country like I had to be burdened with a baby. But you were all that was left of your pa and ma. I had to take you on, burden or no."

I was beginning to wish I hadn't been quite as troublesome over the years as I had been. I wished I'd seen things a little clearer. "I appreciate what you did, Uncle Jack."

"It was the right thing to do. You had a right to some kind of a family, I reckoned." He looked at me and then back out the window. "And I hadn't hardly got started with you, maybe a week into it, still learning my way around diapers and bottles, when one night around six o'clock, I heard this sound at the door, a thump and a little cry, like an animal. Didn't know what it was. Thought it might be a lost cat hungry in the night. Late October it was, and already dark. I went to the door and opened it. This kid was crouched down on the doorstep. Boy, maybe twelve, thirteen."

"My age."

"Just about, I reckon. He tried to stand when I opened the door, but he couldn't. Too weak. Shivering, face covered with sweat, foamy blood around his lips. He looked up at me and whispered, 'Help me. Please help me.'"

Uncle Jack looked at me. Then he turned away again and wiped his hand across his eyes. "Like to kill me every time I think of it," he said. He turned to face me. "Nick, I shut the door."

"Shut the door?"

"Oh, don't get me wrong, Nick. I had to do it. Had to shut that door. I've never doubted that. You

156

were all they had left. If I'd have brought that boy in and you'd have died of the flu, your pa and ma would have haunted me until the day I died. I couldn't have saved that boy. He was a gone goose. But I could have comforted him, made it easier for him while he died. And I would have if it'd been just me. Would have taken the chance. But I couldn't risk you—couldn't. That was the first and last of it. So I shut the door."

He got up, gave himself a shake, and poured himself another cup of coffee.

"He died that night, Uncle Jack?"

"I went looking for him in the morning. I found him a couple of houses up the street, lying at the edge of a yard. I called the undertaker, and we buried him proper."

"How'd you know who he was?"

"He'd written out a little note with his name on it, and his birth date. The undertaker found it in his pocket when they were getting him ready for the burial."

"Who paid for the gravestone?"

"We passed the hat around. Did it a few times to take care of flu victims where they didn't have any families. Old people, mostly."

I sat there, feeling mighty bad about it. Then I said, "Why'd you put that DIED AMONG STRANGERS on his stone? Why not some more normal thing, like GONE TO HIS REWARD or FOUND PEACE AT LAST?"

He sat back and looked out the window into the dark yard. "That was what he wanted. It was on that note in his pocket. Probably hoped he'd live but figured he might die, and he wanted somebody to know that he'd once been around, had existed. If he'd died among his own folks, they'd have hung up a photo of him, or made up an album of his things—school report, photos, stuff like that. I figured he'd want the sadness of himself known." He looked at me again. "I don't know, Nick, it seemed like the right thing to me. Still does."

"You never could find out anything about him?" I said.

"I got the state cops to put out a missing persons check on him, and I got them to run a story in the *Millbury Gazette*."

"That's the story I saw," I said.

"Nothing ever turned up. We figured he must be a runaway. From the slums somewhere. Boston, Portland, who knows. Was having trouble at home, folks broke, drinking, I don't know. Common enough story. Come up here looking for a job on the fishing boats, most likely. Couple of the fishermen thought they might have seen him around the wharf. Caught the flu and that was it."

I got up, found a stub of a pencil in the kitchen drawer, ripped off a corner of the *Gazette*, and started calculating. "The way I figure it, Uncle Jack, on Wednesday I'll be exactly the age he was when he died. To the day."

He looked at me. "I wouldn't make too much of that, Nick." He shrugged and then shook himself. "Well, this isn't getting the dishes done."

I got up and started to clear. I was feeling a lot better than I had. I had plenty to worry about, that was certain. But just understanding it helped. And talking it over with Uncle Jack helped, too. I don't know why it did, but it did.

Chapter Nine

A couple of days later Uncle Jack went over to the court in Millbury to talk to the judge. I wasn't to go; the judge had the doc's report and wanted to have a little chat with Uncle Jack before he decided anything.

"What are you going to tell him?"

"I've been thinking about that, Nick. I guess I'll say there's a kid come to the village who looks a lot like you. I'm not going to say how close he resembles you. Just very similar. That's reasonable enough. Say he's living out in the woods somewhere, coming into the village and stealing, making trouble. People take him for you. Say I've seen the two of you side by side. Won't say anything about the reflection, the gravestone, none of that."

"Do you think the judge will believe you?"

"I don't know. It's reasonable enough to slow him down a little."

The hearing with the judge went just the way Uncle Jack figured. The judge said he'd heard I had always been troublesome—answered back too smart sometimes, hung around with bad companions. "I told the judge that you aren't any worse than a lot of boys, and that you're a good deal better than some I could name. Then he asked me what my intentions are toward Emma Bell. I told him that Emma seems to know more about my intentions than I do, and that I am content as I am and am not in any rush to have intentions toward anyone just yet. Then he showed me the doc's report. He's got the idea that you've got paranoid delusions that were triggered off because you're scared I'm going to marry Emma Bell."

"What's going to happen now?"

"They can't go on one doc's opinion. The judge recognizes that. According to the lawyer, there's some rule about that. You've got to be tested again. We'll see how that comes out. Maybe the next doc'll have more sense than the first one."

A few days later Uncle Jack took me to Millbury to see the new doc. It was the same stuff all over again: what did these black blotches look like, what were the people in pictures talking about, and so forth. This doc brought up the stuff about Uncle Jack getting married to Miss Bell.

I was getting fed up with the whole thing. "Uncle Jack says he hasn't got any intentions toward Miss Bell, so why would I be worried about it?"

"Sometimes we worry about things that aren't real," the doc said.

I knew I shouldn't speak up, but I felt like it. "Not me," I said. "I got enough real things to worry about."

"Oh?" he said, cocking up his eyebrow the way grown-ups do when they think they're going to catch you lying. "Such as what?"

I knew I ought to say something normal, like doing good in school, or whether the other kids liked me, but I was sick of nobody believing me, sick of Miss Bell telling lies about me, sick of these docs asking me dumb questions. "You'd be worried, too, if everybody in town hated you for something you didn't do."

He looked at me with that cocked eye again.

"Then you believe everybody in town hates you, Nick? Everybody's your enemy?"

I was getting myself in deeper, but I didn't care. I didn't see where things could get worse anyway. "Not everybody. Just the dumb jerks like Tumulty and Miss Bell and you."

He frowned, nodded, and wrote something down in his notebook. I didn't care. They could all go jump in the bay as far as I was concerned.

It'd take a few days for him to make up his report and send it to the judge; then they'd have to schedule another hearing. I had a little time. Uncle Jack thought we had a chance, but I didn't. They'd made up their minds that I was evil, and they liked their opinions too well to change them.

So there was nothing for me to do but stay on pins and needles day in and day out; and I was doing just that when I suddenly woke real late a few nights later. For a minute I lay there confused, the way you do when you get waked up, not sure if you're in a dream or not.

Then I realized that some people were downstairs in the parlor talking real loud. I didn't know what time it was, but it felt like two, three in the morning. I heard Uncle Jack's voice say something, but I couldn't make out the words. Somebody else answered back pretty hot, and a couple more chimed in.

I slipped out of bed, crept over to the door, and cracked it open just a hair. A thin stream of pale light came in from the hall. I stuck my head out a little. Somebody said, "Ray Daniels says he came in with his boat just past midnight. He tied up, and by and by he noticed that nobody was standing watch. It was Dauber's turn, he remembered, so he took a walk up the wharf. Then he seen Dauber on the deck of Frankie's *Hobo* out cold as a dead turkey. He says you could of smelled the whiskey from a half mile away. Ray didn't think too much of it, just what you expect of Dauber, but he was blame sore with him for leaving the boats without nobody watching them. He set off for Frankie's house. It took awhile to rouse Frankie up, and maybe a half hour later they come back to the wharf and three of the boats was gone, including the *Hobo* with old man Dauber still out cold on the deck far as anyone knew. Lines was cut. Looked like he used a bolt cutter on them. Just run along the wharf snipping the lines. Oh, the kid had it figured right. Tide was going out, and there was a pretty strong breeze coming off the hills. Them boats was moving out pretty fast."

"Hold up there, Ted," I heard Uncle Jack say. "Nobody actually saw Nick cut those lines. You've got no proof of it."

"Oh yes we do. Eddie Wilson was down there earlier working on his engine. You know that blame clunker of his. He started for home around ten o'clock. On the way he saw Nick coming along towards the wharf, carrying a bottle."

"Eddie's sure it was Nick?"

"Couldn't of missed him. Passed no more'n five feet away. Plenty enough light down there at the wharf for that. Eddie says he didn't think nothin' of it. He knew Nick was friendly with the Daubers and figured he was totin' Dauber a bottle of coffee or something. But it wasn't no coffee."

"Let's go slow here," Uncle Jack said. "Nick hasn't been out of the house all evening. He was here at ten o'clock, because I went upstairs to tell him to shut his light off and go to sleep. He was in bed, reading. Even if he flew down to the wharf, he couldn't have gotten there at ten."

"No use giving us that stuff, Jack. Eddie seen him on the docks with a bottle, and a couple of hours later Dauber was passed out cold. It ain't hard to put it together. And now three boats are gone."

I stood there with my head half out the door, feeling cold, weak, sweat coming out of me every which way. Those fellas loved those boats more than they did their own wives sometimes.

"What about the other two boats?"

"We saved the *Frances II*. Caught up with her near the point—wasn't much damage. But the *Kingfisher*'s all smashed up on the north shore. Worth nothin' but salvage."

"And you can't find the *Hobo*?"

"No. Might spot her in the morning. Could be she's sunk and took Dauber down with her."

Then a voice said, "Now don't try to stand in our way, Jack. We're taking the boy. We can't have no more of this. We're taking him."

"Hold it there, fellas," Uncle Jack said, trying to keep his voice calm. "You can't just take him. You need a warrant. I know this looks bad, but I also know that Nick's been here the whole evening. Wasn't out for five minutes. You go along now, and I promise I'll have Nick down to Tumulty's office first thing tomorrow morning. If Nick did it he'll have to pay for it. But we've got to let the law decide."

"Jack, we already decided. He's got the devil in him. We ain't waitin' for him to do worse than he done already. We ain't waitin' for the law. We got to fix it our own way."

I didn't stand by the door any longer. I scooted across the room as fast as I could move. The window was open. I unhooked the screen and snatched up my pants and shirt from the chair where I'd laid them when I went to bed. I flung the clothes out, fumbled around on the floor until I found shoes and socks, and heaved them out into the yard, too. Then I swung out the window, barefoot, only my shorts on, caught hold of the gutter overhead, worked my way along to the kitchen porch roof, and dropped onto it. I made a good thump, but they were shouting so loud in the house they wouldn't have heard. I figured Uncle Jack was trying to hold them off. A chair crashed over. I swung off the porch roof and dropped to the ground. There was some light falling out the kitchen window into the backyard, enough so I could gather up my clothes. Barefoot, I ran across the yard and slid through the lilac bushes and onto the street. At that hour the houses across the way were dark. I put on my clothes and took a look back at our house. A light snapped on in my bedroom, and there was a shout. I turned and ran as hard as I could up the street, around the corner, and then onto the road heading out toward the Daubers. They were bound to figure I might be heading for the Daubers, but I had to talk to Gypsy.

I went on running until my legs were aching, my lungs red hot, my breath rasping. I slipped off into the woods along the road to rest for a minute, all the time looking back down the road for headlights. Then I set off again at a trot, and pretty soon I came to the Dauber's place.

I crossed the front yard and went around to the kitchen door. I knew it wouldn't be locked—they'd lost the key a long time ago. Over in the east the sky was getting just the faintest bit light—four-thirty, five o'clock in the morning maybe. I slid the kitchen door open and went in. I was glad there was a little light, for I could see the shapes of the chairs and table well enough to skirt around them. I worked my way through the kitchen and opened the door to the little room off it where Gypsy slept. I eased the door open, knelt by her bed, and put my hand over her mouth. I whispered, "Gypsy, it's Nick. Don't make any noise."

For a little bit she struggled. Then she woke up enough to figure out what was going on. I took my hand off her mouth. "I can't stay, Gypsy. I got to make a run for it. The other me cut three boats loose from the wharf. One of them got all smashed up on the north shore."

She sat up. "He cut boats loose?"

"Yes. He had it figured right. There was a pretty good breeze blowing offshore and it carried the boats out into the bay pretty fast."

"They all got smashed?"

"No." I didn't want to tell her, but I had to. "They caught up to one of them before it hit the rocks. The other one's missing. Blown out to sea, maybe. Or capsized and sunk."

"Which boat?"

I took a deep breath. "The *Hobo*."

"The *Hobo*? The one Pa was working on?"

"Yes. Gypsy, your pa was on it. *Is* on it." I took another breath. "Most likely still afloat. Jared brought him a bottle of whiskey. He was on deck out cold when Jared cut the boat loose. Probably okay. He may have woken up by now and brought her in safe somewhere."

"You mean he might have drowned?"

"No. I don't think so. Not your pa. He's too tough to drown." Then I heard the distant sound of a car. "I got to run for it, Gypsy. Meet me at our place tomorrow at dusk. Make blame sure nobody follows you."

She grabbed on to me. "Do you think Pa didn't get drowned?"

"Sure of it. He's too tough."

She wouldn't let go of me. "Pa can't be drowned, Nick. He can't be." Her voice was loud and wailing.

"Stop hollering. When they come in, tell them you haven't seen me for a couple of days." I jerked loose and ran out through the kitchen. As I did so, headlights swung across the front lawn. It was just a hair lighter now, and I could make out the shapes of trees and such. I raced across the barnyard, past the truck garden. Beyond the garden was a stand of hardwoods. I'd never make any time through them in the dark. I cut back onto the dusty road and stopped to take a quick look around.

Back at the house I heard a couple of car doors slam, and a light went on in the house. I started off again up the road, running hard. My legs were tired, my lungs rasping, but scared as I was, I hardly noticed. I just kept on running, sucking in air until

I smelled the pine forest on both sides of the road.

I stopped. It was getting light enough to see the trees. Then I heard the faint sound of a car engine. I ducked off into the pines and started upward into the hills. It was pretty dark in amongst the pine trees, and I couldn't make much time, but I knew they wouldn't even try to come in there after me until it got full daylight. I was safe for now.

The sun was coming up. I went on more slowly now, picking my way over fallen trees, up ledges, down into gulches. They'd probably get dogs after me, but it'd take them time to get hold of the right dogs. There was an awful lot of pine forest to cover up in these hills. I could be miles away by afternoon.

Going slower I had a little chance to think about the mess I was in. It was a whole lot worse than before. Then they'd just wanted to get rid of me—got the devil in me and was likely to cause trouble. But now it was about their boats. Then didn't want to get rid of me anymore. They wanted to kill me. Wanted revenge. Wanted to hang me from a big tree limb. Maybe not even take that much trouble, but shoot me down on sight. Some of those fellas had been hunting up in these hills all their lives. Could kill me at two hundred yards. More, maybe. Catch me up here in the hills four, five miles from town, bury me up here and tell everybody they never saw me, that I must have run off to another state.

Maybe I'd have to do that. Go across the hills and down the other side to some town where nobody knew me. Make it to Portland, Boston, some other place.

I sure didn't want to do that. Never see Uncle Jack again, never see the sun shining on the bay, never swim in Briggs Pond, never go with Gypsy to our secret place. But maybe I would have to.

Suddenly I felt awful tired. I looked around for a log and sat down. It seemed like I was running out of hopes. I kept looking everywhere for a way out— a door here, and a door there, but they were all closed in my face. There was no hope for me anywhere. But I was too tired to think about it any-more, so I crawled off into a cluster of small pines where nobody would see me from five feet away, lay down, and went to sleep.

When I woke up, the sun was high in the sky— close to noon, I figured. For a while I lay there listening for the sound of dogs or people: nothing but the wind in the pine boughs, the chirps and cheeps of birds and squirrels. I was still mighty scared, but hungry, too, for I hadn't had anything to eat since supper—no breakfast, no lunch. I figured Gypsy would bring some food with her when she came tonight, for she usually had food on her mind. But she might not come after all—might be some fishermen out there keeping an eye on her.

I still hadn't decided what to do. Best to wait until I saw Gypsy that night and got a better idea of what was going on. Maybe Uncle Jack had gotten them to ease off. Maybe they'd found the *Hobo*. There were all kinds of maybes.

I figured I'd better get something to eat if I could find anything, so I set off in search of blueberries, which you were likely to find in clearings, and by luck a half hour later I came across a clearing with three blueberry bushes in it. I was standing there by the bushes, ramming the berries into my mouth as fast as I could pick them, when I heard the faint sound of an airplane engine. I looked up. No sign of a plane—just blue sky and some fluffy white clouds.

I waited. The sound was coming closer. Quickly I snatched at a few more berries, then dashed out of the clearing and back into the shadow of the pines. The plane kept coming, pretty low. I waited. Then it crossed over the clearing, its shadow flashing through the blueberry bushes. I peered upward at the plane through the pines. The pine branches blocked my view some, but I could see enough of the plane—a little yellow job flying real low. Were they hunting for me? Or was it just some plane flying somewhere? I waited. The plane went off north, the engine noise dying down. Then the engine sound changed, and I knew the plane was coming back toward me. I lay down in the shadows, my face hidden. The plane came over again, went off south a ways, then circled back, this time passing over the pines a bit farther to the east. There wasn't any doubt of it now: they were hunting for me.

That was bad: they were making a big thing of it. If Mr. Dauber had drowned, they'd have me up for murder. Unless the fishermen in Stoneybeach got to me first. If you were wanted for murder, they printed pictures of you in the newspapers so everybody knew what you looked like. Mighty hard to slip away to another place.

Lying there in the pines, I felt cold and sweaty and lonely as could be. What had I done? I wanted to cry, but I wouldn't let myself.

Then there came a sound out of the ordinary— not the *crek-crek* of a squirrel nor the cheep of a bird. I couldn't say exactly what the sound was, but it wasn't natural. I lay there waiting. The sound came again—a sort of scraping noise. I raised my head and looked around. Couldn't see anything but pine trees. I knelt up. "Jared," I said, not too loud, in case there were fishermen out there somewhere.

The sound stopped. I stood and then I saw him. He was about ten feet up in a pine tree a few yards away, half hidden amongst the branches. I started to run zig-zag toward him as hard as I could through the pines. He put his arms around the trunk of the tree and slid down with that scraping sound. When he hit the ground, he started to run off through the pincs.

"Jared," I called. "Wait. I have something to tell you."

He stopped running and turned around to face me. He was crouched a little, ready to run if I made a move toward him. It was mighty strange to see myself half crouched amongst the pines—my own face, my own body, my own clothes. "Why'd you call me Jared?' he said.

"Uncle Jack told me what happened—about you knocking on our door, the note in your pocket, and all that. I'm sorry about it."

"Too late to be sorry for that now, isn't it, Nick? Too late for that." He spit into the pine needles.

"Even so, it wasn't any of my doing. Why are you blaming me?"

He saw now that I wasn't going to rush him, and he straightened up out of his crouch and hooked his thumbs into his belt the way I always did. "Why do I care who's to blame? Wait till they bring your body home to your uncle full of bullets. Wait till he sees that. He'll get a good laugh out of that, I reckon."

"So you agree that it wasn't my fault."

"Oh no. Not so fast, Nick Hodges. Why should you have gotten saved and I didn't? Whose fault was that?"

"If you tell me who your folks are, I could let them know what happened."

"Them," he said. "Them. Nice, happy folks, they were. Ready to do anything for anyone at the drop of a hat, they were. Couldn't wait to rush in and be helpful." He shook his fist. "Them."

I changed the subject. "Look, whatever Uncle Jack did, he went to a lot of trouble and expense to see that you were buried proper and got a gravestone."

"Just what every thirteen-year-old boy wants for Christmas, a gravestone." That struck him as funny, and he began to dance. "Merry Christmas to all and to all a good night."

"Listen," I said. "I've been figuring. You were thirteen years, three months, and six days the night you . . . turned up on our doorstep. Right?"

He stopped dancing and I could see his breath coming hard. "So what?"

"I'm exactly that old today. You mean to take the rest of my life for yourself?"

His face was whipping around like waves in a storm. "Oh yes, and I'm going to, going to. Oh yes, I'm going to." He turned and disappeared into the pine forest. I had no chance of catching him—he'd gotten too much of a jump on me. But it didn't really matter, for now I knew he was tracking me around the woods, waiting for his chance to let the people of Stoneybeach know where I was. And then an idea came to me. It was a mighty risky idea, all right, but it gave me a chance.

Chapter Ten

I waited out the day, and when the sun started to go down through the pines, I made my way back down the hills toward me and Gypsy's place. I went real slow, stopping to listen every five minutes or so. It took me awhile to get down out of the hills, and by the time I got to our place, it was dusk. I lay back in the pines about fifty feet, looking through the dusk and listening. By and by I heard a sound, and Gypsy came into the clearing and sat down on our log. I stood, and moving in a crouch I circled out to the road and lay there for a long while, looking and listening. Finally I was satisfied and went back into the woods. "Hey, Gypsy," I said in a low voice.

She jumped up. "Where?"

"Back here."

She scrambled into the woods and gave me a hug. Then we worked our way farther back a hundred yards or so and sat on the ground. She had a paper bag with her. "Here," she said. "I figured you'd be hungry."

"I could eat a horse. I haven't had anything to eat but blueberries all day." I reached into the bag. There were a couple of ham sandwiches and about half a cake.

"I made the cake myself," Gypsy said. "Ma's too upset to cook."

It was the heaviest piece of cake I'd ever lifted, but I wasn't about to complain. "They didn't find your pa?"

"No. Nor the *Hobo* neither. They say it might be sunk and Pa's got drowned. They got a murder warrant out for you."

That didn't surprise me. "I wouldn't worry about your pa," I said. "He isn't planning on turning up until he finishes that bottle Jared brought him." However, I wasn't so sure about it. Good chance he was drowned. Even if the *Hobo* hadn't gone down, he might have fallen off. But I didn't say that. "Did you tell the police you hadn't seen me?"

"They didn't ask me, they asked Ma. She didn't know you was there. They stuck around for a while, figuring you might come, but when you didn't, they left. State police guy came this afternoon and asked questions, but he left, too. There's nobody home now but Ma. She can't stop crying. She's like a water faucet. Nick, I don't want Pa to be drowned. I couldn't stand it."

It surprised me. "How come you and your ma are so worked up about it? I thought you wanted to be rid of him."

"Oh, but not drowned, Nick. I never wanted him dead."

"Well, he's probably okay." I had more things on my minds than Mr. Dauber. "Listen, have you heard any talk about me? What they're planning to do and all?"

"Talk about you? You're all the talk. That's all everybody wants to talk about. It's on the radio, Nick. You were on the radio." She was pretty impressed by that.

But I wasn't. In ordinary times I'd have been tickled to be on the radio—make Barnes, Santini, and the rest listen and boast about it in school afterward. But this time I wasn't so happy about it.

"What'd they say?"

"Oh, it's a big thing. They say you're crazy. They got one of them docs on and he said you was—I don't remember the word."

"What else?"

"Oh, you're mighty dangerous and people should keep their doors locked and not let strangers in."

They'd blown everything up to about ten times the size it ought to have been. "It makes me sick," I said.

She looked at me, her eyes wide, scared for me, but impressed that I'd gotten to be so important. "Nick, will they shoot you?"

"Some of them want to. They might if they get a chance. If they saw me and I started to run, they probably would."

"What're you going to do, Nick?"

I began eating the sandwich. "I don't know, Gypsy," I said. That wasn't true. I knew what I was going to do, but I didn't want to say anything: I figured Jared Solters was out there in the pines keeping an eye on me and might be close enough to hear us talking. "They'll bring the dogs in pretty soon. Once they get the dogs, I won't have much of a chance."

"Then you better get away from Stoneybeach. Go

someplace else until things cool down."

I shook my head. "Things aren't going to cool down around here for a long while, Gypsy. I could come back twenty years from now and they'd still go after me."

"Well, you better go someplace, Nick."

I shook my head again. "If they're talking about me on the radio, they'll have my picture in the papers. Bound to."

"Where'll they get a picture?"

"They've got some at school. That photographer who comes every year takes pictures of all the kids in hopes the parents will buy some. Even Uncle Jack bought some to send out to Ma's cousins at Christmas one year. I've thought about it. If I run off, I'll have to find a job right away. Won't be able to eat if I don't. Some thirteen-year-old kid turns up somewhere looking for a job, first thing people are going to think of is the kid who murdered a lot of people over in Stoneybeach. Look up my picture."

We were quiet for a bit. Then she said, "I wish I could help, Nick."

"I wish you could, too. But they're bound to be suspicious of anything you do."

"They are already. They all know Pa hit us when

he got tanked up. They figure I was in on it to get rid of him. Figured I found Pa's whiskey and sent you down with it. They don't know Pa—it'd take a bloodhound to find where he hid his whiskey. They hate us. They'll blame us for anything."

It was true. It didn't seem like there was anything we could do about that, either. To cheer her up I said, "Don't you worry, Gypsy. I'll think of something."

Much as I wanted to be with Gypsy, so as to hold off the loneliness, I knew I shouldn't linger: Jared might already be luring people after me. So I wrapped up the rest of the cake for breakfast and walked back into the hills through the pine forest a couple of miles. I was dead tired. They wouldn't try to find me in the dark; there was too much woods for that. At night amongst the pines you could walk within a foot of somebody and never see him. And if they came up in a posse with dogs and lights, the commotion would wake me before they got within a mile of me.

Where was Jared? I sat there, putting myself in his shoes. His big problem was that nobody in the village could tell him from me. Show himself and they'd be after him in two shakes. But he had to show himself enough so that they'd start after him. Then he could lead them toward me and disappear. I didn't know exactly how he would make himself disappear, but I didn't doubt that he could.

I was too tired to think about it anymore, so I curled up tight against myself to stay warm and went to sleep.

I woke up at the first sun. I searched around until I found a little stream, for I wasn't going to try to eat that cake without anything to wash it down. I scrubbed myself up a little in the cold stream water, finished off the cake, and then started down through the pine forest towards Briggs Pond. I pretended to go quiet and easy, but every once in awhile I'd kick a stone or step on a branch and snap it, like it was an accident. I figured I probably didn't have to do that; he was probably following me anyway. But I wanted to be sure he was.

So I went down, and by and by there was light coming through the pines at the east. I pushed on a little bit, and then I lay flat. Through the pines I could see bits and pieces of Briggs Pond, the blue water sparkling a little in the sunshine. They'd mowed the field that surrounded the pond a little while before. Farther away, at the other end of the pond, was the road that ran from Stoneybeach over to Millbury. Every once in awhile a car went by, raising dust. Mighty peaceful, if I didn't know better. I lay down and pretended I was going to sleep.

He'd wait me out for a while—see if I was really asleep. How long, I didn't know. Hard to guess. Try to hold himself down, hold himself back, but in the end he'd get worried that I'd wake up and leave.

So I waited, listening carefully for his movements. It was amazing how many sounds there were out there. Little birds chirping and whistling, squirrels going click-click-click, crows up in the treetops cawing, chipmunks quarreling across the pine floor. Plenty going on, and it was hard to hear Jared's movements.

But then I heard a little slushing sound. I waited. It came again. He was sliding along to get a closer look at me. I went on lying still and waited. A couple of minutes later I heard him slide away again. I waited some more until I was sure he was gone, and then I sat up and looked around. Nothing to see.

How long would it take? It was about fifteen minutes along the road to where the houses began —I knew, for I'd walked it often enough. Then maybe another five minutes or so until he got into the middle of the village—if he got that far before somebody recognized him. He'd get back here a lot quicker, for he'd be running as fast as he could.

I waited. Then I heard a little sound, coming and going with the breeze—so faint I couldn't tell what kind of sound it was, just a sound. My heart began to pump. I raised up on my knees to look through the pines. Nothing to see, just that sound.

Quickly it grew to a murmur, nothing I could make much out of, just a murmur, but there all right. I stood and went to the edge of the pines where I could get a clean view of things. The sun flashed on the pond, and there were still clumps of brown grass in the field around it that the hay rake had missed.

I crouched. The murmur was more distinct. There were shouts coming out of the murmur, like a tall man in a crowd. "There he goes. Over there." Jared had got a good start on them—showed himself in a shop or on the street, and then taken off for the pond. He was probably cutting through the woods and fields alongside the road, showing himself just enough to keep them coming, and then ducking out of sight.

I waited, my breath coming hard, my heart racing, the sweat dripping down my side under my shirt. The murmuring was now mostly shouts. Then Jared burst out of a little piece of woods that bordered on the field around the pond. He was running hard, directly toward me. Almost at the same moment I saw the mob of people running along the road. When they got to the pond, they saw Jared running up toward me. A roar rose out of them, like the sound of an animal after its kill, and the mob came running after Jared across the field, all bunched together like a huge creature with a hundred legs.

Jared looked over his shoulder but kept running toward me. By now, he figured, I would be running myself, heading on up into the hills. But I wasn't going to be. Instead, I burst out of the pine forest and ran straight at him.

When he saw me, he stopped dead in his tracks. His mouth fell open and he looked wildly around. The roaring animal was only a hundred feet behind him. I went on charging toward him. He turned to look behind him, then back at me. And then he started to charge for the pond.

But I was on him. I tackled him and we both went

down in a heap, kicking and clawing at each other. He jerked his legs free and jumped to his feet. I jumped up, too, and we stood face to face, not more than a yard apart. I grabbed at him, but he was too quick for me. He charged for the lake, dove, and disappeared.

The mob veered away from me to run to the lake. They stood there, waiting for him to come up. But I knew he wouldn't, and I waited until they realized it, too.

Then I heard Frank Sanders say, "Glory be, there was two of them after all."

I walked to the water, waiting for the ripples to die down. After a bit they did, and there I saw, amid the reflection of the sky and clouds, the reflection of myself.

Epilogue

Of course they dragged the pond, looking for his body, but I knew they wouldn't find anything, and they didn't. I was just as glad, for I didn't want anybody to know the truth of it—bad enough having a reputation for being troublesome without them thinking I was bewitched or something. Of course Uncle Jack knew, but he had sense enough not to say anything, and Gypsy knew, but nobody would believe anything she said, much less this.

So the story went around that there had been this runaway kid who looked a lot like Nick Hodges, sleeping in barns and cellars. Most likely wasn't right in the head. Stealing and causing trouble. Had probably gotten into trouble at home, which was why he ran off in the first place. A few people blamed poor Nick for it for awhile, but everything turned out all right. Constable Tumulty sent out an inquiry around the state for missing kids, but nothing turned up. There was some talk about draining the pond to find the body, but that was bound to be an expense, and the idea was dropped.

The *Hobo* turned up a couple of days later. Mr. Dauber had woken up that morning at first light to find himself at sea. He started the boat up, but instead of running it back to Stoneybeach right away, he took it into the fishing village closest to where he was, traded an anchor for a bottle of whiskey, and stayed aboard drinking until another fisherman from Stoneybeach spotted the boat. Of course Mr. Dauber claimed he didn't know anything about the anchor, most likely somebody stole it when he was asleep, but nobody believed him. It put an end to his career as a fisherman.

Later on, Gypsy and I sat behind the barn and talked it over. "What's your pa going to do now?"

She shrugged. "He says there's jobs upstate. He figures he can catch on up there. He's soured on Stoneybeach. People here are nothin' but snobs, he says. Won't never give a man a break."

"You think he'll do it, Gypsy?"

"Sure. It'll last a couple of weeks. Month maybe. Then he'll turn up here again, wanting his dinner." She handed me a piece of the pie she'd swiped. "Did anyone say they were sorry for what happened, Nick?"

"No. Constable Tumulty said it was a natural mistake, anyone could have made it, and it was half my own fault for being troublesome in the first place. He advised me not to spend so much time with you."

"Oh yeah?" she said through a mouthful of pie. "It wasn't me that tried to hang anybody."

"They pretty much forgot about that. Said a few people went a little overboard with it. Said Constable Tumulty made too much out of it, maybe, but that was his job."

Gypsy swallowed a chunk of pie. "So they're going to forget about the whole thing? Like it never happened?"

"I reckon so. Looks like it, anyway. If they could forget about the flu epidemic, they can forget about this. I don't guess you ever learn very much by forgetting things, but Uncle Jack says maybe it's for the best."

She stood up. "One thing I learned a long time ago, if I don't get them chickens in, Ma'll learn me something on my rear end."

I stood up, and we went after the chickens. "You fools," I said. "Can't you ever learn anything? You're no smarter than human beings."